THE HEN WHO DREAMED SHE COULD FLY

"Everything wonderful about the world is contained in this small gem of a novel, which brims with dream-fulfilling adventures and the longing that underlies love."

—Kyung-sook Shin, author of the *New York Times* bestseller *Please Look After Mom*

"*The Hen Who Dreamed She Could Fly* breaks down the boundaries between the animal and the human and takes us on the intensely personal journey of a lonely hen whose simple, fierce desires guide her to surprising places. This entertaining and plaintive tale is South Korea's *Charlotte's Web* for youth and adults alike." —Krys Lee, author of *Drifting House*

"An adroit allegory about life . . . in the vein of classics like *Charlotte's Web* and *Jonathan Livingston Seagull* . . . A subtle morality tale that will appeal to readers of all ages."

—*Kirkus Reviews*

"[A] simply told but absorbing fable . . . Spare but evocative line drawings . . . add to the subtle charm." —*Publishers Weekly*

"Recalling *Jonathan Livingston Seagull*, this slim but powerful tale will resonate with readers of all ages, who can take it at face value or delve deeper into its meditations on living courageously and facing mortality. . . The English translation moves smoothly and straightforwardly and is aided by graceful black-and-white illustrations." —*Booklist*

THE HEN WHO DREAMED SHE COULD FLY

© Kwon Yongsang

SUN-MI HWANG is a beloved writer in South Korea, where she has won many awards and published more than forty books enjoyed by adults and children alike. Born in 1963, she was unable to attend middle school due to poverty, but thanks to a teacher who gave her a key to a classroom, she could go to the school and read books whenever she wanted. She enrolled in high school by taking a certificate examination, and she graduated from the creative writing departments at Seoul Institute of the Arts and Gwangju University, and from the graduate school of Chung-Ang University. She lives in Seoul, South Korea.

Upon its publication in 2000, *The Hen Who Dreamed She Could Fly* became an instant classic, remaining on bestseller lists for ten years and inspiring the highest-grossing animated film in Korean history. It has also been adapted into a comic book, a play, and a musical, and has been translated into over a dozen languages.

CHI-YOUNG KIM is the translator of the *New York Times* bestselling Korean novel *Please Look After Mom* by Kyung-sook Shin. She lives in Los Angeles, California.

NOMOCO is a Japanese designer and illustrator based in London. She has exhibited her work in solo and group exhibitions in London, Milan, Tokyo, Singapore, and New York. She also produces work under her full name, Kazuko Nomoto.

THE HEN WHO DREAMED
SHE COULD FLY

Sun-mi Hwang

Translated by Chi-Young Kim

Illustrations by Nomoco

ONEWORLD

A Oneworld Book

First published in Great Britain and the Commonwealth by
Oneworld Publications 2014
Reprinted in 2014

Published by arrangement with Penguin Books, a division of Penguin Group
(USA) LLC, A Penguin Random House Company

Copyright © 2000 by Sun-mi Hwang

Translation copyright © 2013 by Chi-Young Kim

The moral right of Sun-mi Hwang to be identified as the Author of this work
has been asserted by her in accordance with the Copyright, Designs, and Patents
Act 1988

Illustrations by Nomoco

Originally published in Korean as *Madangeul naon amtak*
by Sakyejul Publishing Ltd, Seoul

The Hen Who Dreamed She Could Fly is published with the support of Literature
Translation Institute of Korea (LTI Korea)

All rights reserved
Copyright under Berne Convention
A CIP record for this title is available from the British Library

ISBN 978-1-78074-534-3
ISBN 978-1-78074-535-0 (eBook)

Set in Adobe Jensen Pro
Designed by Sabrina Bowers
Printed and bound by CPI Group (UK) Ltd, Croydon, CR0 4YY

This is a work of fiction. While, as in all fiction, the literary perceptions and
insights are based on experience, all names, characters, places, and incidents
either are products of the author's imagination or are
used fictitiously.

Oneworld Publications
10 Bloomsbury Street
London WC1B 3SR
England

Visit our website for a reading guide
and exclusive content on
The Hen Who Dreamed She Could Fly
www.oneworld-publications/hen

CONTENTS

THE HEN WHO DREAMED
SHE COULD FLY

I REFUSE
TO LAY ANOTHER EGG!

T he egg rolled to a stop upon reaching the wire mesh of the coop. Sprout looked at it—a chalky egg flecked with blood. She hadn't laid an egg in two days; she doubted she could anymore. Yet there it was—one small, sad egg.

This cannot happen again, she thought. Would the farmer's wife take it? She'd collected all the others, complaining every time that they were getting smaller and smaller. She wouldn't leave this one behind just because it was ugly, would she?

Sprout couldn't even stand upright today. No wonder—somehow she had managed to lay an egg without having eaten a thing. Sprout wondered how many eggs she had left inside her; she hoped this was the last one. With a sigh she peered outside. Because her cage was near the entrance she could see out beyond the wire mesh walls. The door to the coop didn't quite fit its frame; through the gap she could see an acacia tree. Sprout loved that tree so much, she didn't complain about the cold winter wind that made it through the gap, or the pelting summer rain.

Sprout was an egg-laying hen, which meant she was raised for her eggs. She had come to the coop over a year before. Since then, all she had done was lay eggs. She couldn't wander around, flap her wings, or even sit on her own eggs. She had never stepped outside the coop. But ever since she had seen a hen running around the yard with the adorable chicks she had hatched, Sprout had harbored a secret desire—to hatch an egg and watch the birth of her chick. But it was an impossible dream. The coop was tilted forward so the eggs would roll to the other side of a barrier, separating them from their mothers.

The door opened, and in came the farmer, pushing a wheelbarrow. The hens clucked impatiently, creating a din.

"Breakfast!"

"I'm hungry, hurry hurry!"

With a bucket, the farmer scooped out the feed. "Always so hungry! You better make it worth it. This feed isn't cheap."

Sprout looked through the wide-open door, focusing on the world outside. It had been a while since she'd had an appetite. She had no desire to lay another egg. Her heart emptied of feeling every time the farmer's wife took her eggs. The pride she felt when she laid one was replaced by sadness. She was exhausted after a full year of this. She couldn't so much as touch her own eggs, not even with the tip of her foot. And she didn't know what happened to them after the farmer's wife carried them in her basket out of the coop.

It was bright outside. The acacia tree on the edge of the yard was blooming with white flowers. Their sweet scent caught the breeze and wafted into the coop, filling Sprout's heart. Sprout got up and shoved her head through the wires of her cage. Her bare, featherless neck was rubbed raw. *The leaves laid flowers again!* Sprout was envious. If she squinted, she could make out the light green leaves that had matured and given birth to fragrant flowers. She'd spotted the blooming acacia tree the very day she was shut in the coop. A few days later, the tree shed its flowers, which flew around like snowflakes, leaving behind green leaves. The leaves lived on until late fall before turning yellow and then dropping quietly. Sprout was awestruck as she watched the leaves stand strong against rough winds and heavy rain before fading and falling. When she saw them reborn in light green the following spring, she was overcome with excitement.

Sprout was the best name in the world. A sprout grew into a leaf and embraced the wind and the sun before falling and rotting and turning into mulch for bringing fragrant flowers into bloom. Sprout wanted to do something with her life, just like the sprouts on the acacia tree. That was why she'd named herself after them. Nobody called her Sprout, and she knew her life wasn't like a sprout's, but still the name made her feel good. It was her secret. Ever since she'd named herself, she'd gotten into the habit of noting the events occurring outside the coop: everything from the moon waxing and waning and the sun rising and setting to the animals in the barnyard bickering.

"Go on, eat so you can lay lots of big eggs!" the farmer bellowed. He said this every time he fed the hens, and Sprout was sick of hearing it. She gazed into the yard, ignoring him.

The animals out there were busy eating breakfast. A large family of ducks surrounded a trough with their tails pointing up to the sky, swallowing their food without once raising their heads. The old dog was nearby, stuffing himself. He may have his own bowl, but he had to scarf down all his food before the rooster got wind of it. Once, he refused to let the rooster eat out of his bowl and received a vicious pecking that drew blood from his muzzle. The rooster and hen's trough wasn't crowded. Because they didn't have any offspring right now, they were the only ones who could eat leisurely. Even so, the rooster still showed interest in the old dog's bowl. He cemented his status as the leader of the barn by refusing to back off even when the dog lowered his tail and growled. He was handsome, with a tall, awe-inspiring tail, a bright red comb, a fearless gaze, and a sharp beak. It fell to him to crow at dawn, and after that he would saunter around the fields with the hen.

Whenever she saw the yard hen, Sprout couldn't stand it—she felt even more confined in her wire cage. She, too, wanted to dig through the pile of compost with the rooster, walk side by side with him, and sit on her eggs. She couldn't get to the yard where the ducks and the old dog and the rooster and the hen lived together no matter how far she stretched her neck through the wires; they just plucked her feathers. *Why am I in the coop when that hen is out in the yard?* She didn't know that the rooster and the hen were organically raised native Korean chickens. Nor did she know that an egg she laid on her own would never hatch, no matter how long she sat on it. If she'd known that, she might never have begun dreaming of hatching one.

The ducks finished eating and filed under the acacia tree, waddling toward the nearby hill, trailed by a slightly smaller bird with different coloring. His head was green like an acacia leaf—maybe he wasn't a duck. But then again, he quacked and waddled. Sprout didn't know how a mallard duck had come to live in the yard, she just knew he looked different. She was still gazing outside when the farmer came up to feed her. He cocked his head as he noticed the previous day's feed still in her trough. "Huh? What's going on here?" he muttered. He usually left after pouring the feed, to be followed by his wife collecting the eggs. But today he was doing her job. "Not eating at all these days. Must be sick." The farmer tutted, then glanced at Sprout with displeasure. He reached down to pick up her egg. As soon as his fingers touched it, it gave way; thin wrinkles rippled across its surface. Sprout was shocked. She knew it was small and ugly, but she had never imagined it would be soft. The shell hadn't even finished hardening! The farmer frowned.

Sprout felt her heart tearing in two. Her sorrow each time her eggs were taken away was nothing compared to how she felt now. Sobs filled her throat; her entire body stiffened. *Poor thing came out without a shell.* The farmer tossed the soft egg into the yard; bracing herself, Sprout squeezed her eyes shut. The egg broke without a sound. The old dog lumbered over to lick it up. Tears flowed freely from Sprout's eyes for the first time in her life. *I refuse to lay another egg! Ever!*

FLYING THE COOP

Sprout liked to stare out into the barnyard. She would much rather watch the ducks scuttle away from the dog than peck at feed. Closing her eyes, she imagined herself wandering freely about. She fantasized about sitting in a nest, on an egg, about venturing into the fields with the rooster, and about following the ducks around. She sighed. It was pointless to dream. It would never happen to her. She had not been able to lay an egg for the past few days. This was no surprise, since she could barely get to her feet.

On the fifth day without an egg, Sprout woke up from a deep sleep to hear the farmer's wife grousing, "We need to cull it. Take it out of the coop." Sprout had never thought she would leave the coop. She didn't understand the word "cull," but the thought of getting out of the coop gave her a burst of energy. She lifted her head with effort and sipped some water. The next day, too, she failed to lay an egg. Sprout could sense it—her body could no longer make eggs. But she still took in a bit of water and feed. She couldn't wait for her new life to begin. She would hatch an egg and raise a chick. She could do it if she could only get out into the yard. She waited, brimming with anticipation. She slept fitfully, imagining playing in the fields with the rooster and scratching at the ground.

The following day, the door to the coop opened and the farmer and his wife entered, pushing an empty wheelbarrow. Sprout was so weak she couldn't stand up straight, but mentally she was sharper than ever before. She raised her voice for the first time in a long while: "I'm flying the coop!" she clucked. The most wonderful day since she was shut in the coop had dawned. The scent of the acacias filled the air.

"We can probably get something for the meat, right?" the farmer's wife asked her husband.

"I'm not sure. It looks sickly. . . ."

Their conversation didn't register with Sprout, whose heart pounded at the thought that she would finally live in the yard. The farmer grabbed her by the wings and pulled her out of her cramped cage. Sprout landed with a thud in the wheelbarrow. She was too weak to resist or even to flap her wings. She craned her neck but for only a moment. Then other weak hens landed on top of her, smothering Sprout. In a separate wire cage, the farmer and his wife loaded up old hens whose egg-bearing years were behind them but who were otherwise healthy, then loaded them into a truck that drove off the farm. Sprout remained in the wheelbarrow, weighed down by hens on the verge of death. The last hen landed on her head. Sprout was scared. She tried not to lose consciousness, wondering what was happening. The loud clucks gradually died down, and soon she couldn't hear a thing. It was getting difficult to breathe. *Is this what it means to be culled?* Sprout's eyelids drooped. *I can't die like this.* She tried to muster up courage but grew only more frightened. Sorrow bubbled up from the bottom of her heart. She couldn't die like this, not before getting to the yard. She had to escape from the wheelbarrow. But the hens stacked on top of her were crushing her bones.

Sprout focused on the image of the acacia tree blooming with flowers, the green leaves, the wonderful scent, and the happy animals in the yard. She had only one wish, to hatch an egg and watch the birth of a chick. It was an ordinary wish, but now she was dying before she could fulfill it. As her consciousness wavered, Sprout began to see things. She saw herself sitting on an egg, warming it in a nest. The noble rooster stood guard at her side and acacia flowers fluttered down like snow. *I've always wanted to hatch an egg. Just once! One egg just for me. I've wanted to whisper, I won't ever leave you, Baby. Go on, crack the shell, I want to meet you. Don't be scared, Baby! And cuddle my baby upon birth.* Believing she was really incubating an egg, she lost consciousness, a smile on her beak.

Sprout opened her eyes. How much time had passed? It was raining, and she was soaked to the bone. She didn't know where she was. *I guess I didn't die.* She was freezing. Even after her mind cleared, she couldn't move. She would feel better if she shook her feathers out, but she didn't have the strength.

She heard something from above. Only after that noise repeated itself did she understand.

"Hey, you. Can you hear me?" the voice called.

Sprout managed to lift her head. She could smell a terrible odor but couldn't see what was around her.

"You're fine. I knew it!" The excited voice grew louder. "Get up! Take a step!"

"Take a step? I can't. It's too hard." Sprout looked around at the trees on the dusky slope and the grass dancing in the wind on top of the dike. From somewhere over there she heard the voice again.

"You're not dead. Come on, get up!"

"Of course I'm not dead." Sprout flexed her wings and stretched her legs and shook her neck to and fro. Everything was intact; she was just weak. "Who are you?"

"Stop talking. You need to run away. Hurry!"

Sprout staggered to her feet. It took everything she had to take a few steps toward the voice. When was the last time she'd walked? One step, two steps. She froze in place, then sat down, stunned. "Oh, my god. What is this?"

Dead hens were piled all around her. She was stepping on them. She was stuck in a large open grave.

"But I'm still alive! How can this be?" Sprout sprang up and ran around, clucking in panic. But she couldn't escape. She trod on corpses with every step she took. Her terror was bottomless. She couldn't believe her eyes.

"What in the world are you doing?" the voice asked from beyond the grave.

But Sprout was too busy running around and clucking. "Oh, no! What am I going to do?"

"Watch out, be careful!"

"I'm not dead! How can this be?"

"Look over there. You're being targeted!"

"What am I going to do? What am I going to do?"

"Run away! Can't you see you're a target? You dumb hen! Those eyes are on you!" the voice hollered.

Only then did Sprout stop making a fuss. Something was slinking in the grass opposite from where the voice was coming. Two eyes were glaring at her. A chill shot down her spine.

"If you stay there you're going to get into trouble!"

Sprout didn't know who was ordering her around from outside the open grave but decided he was more trustworthy than the glinting eyes. "You must be the rooster!" she cried. Only he would have the courage to shout in the dark like this. Sprout followed the voice to the edge of the grave. The hole was shallower there, so she was able to hop out easily.

"Good job," her new friend said in a calm, kind voice.

Sprout shuddered and took a good look at her friend. It was the mallard duck from the yard—the mallard with extraordinary green and brown feathers, the loner who always trailed the family of ducks. It began to sink in that she had indeed left the chicken coop. "Thank you for saving me!"

"No need to thank me. I couldn't let him get you. When he gets someone alive, I get so unbelievably angry."

"Who?"

"The weasel!" The mallard shuddered, his neck feathers bristling.

Sprout trembled, too. The weasel stood proudly on the other side of the open grave. He was glaring at them, angry that his meal had escaped.

"Go back, now that you survived," the mallard said and waddled off.

"Wait, where?" The mallard wasn't planning to take her along! She wanted to follow him into the yard. Why would she go back? "I'm not going back to the coop. I just got out! I was culled."

"Culled? What does that mean?"

"I'm not sure, but I think it means I'm free."

"In any case it's dangerous to stay here. Just go. I'm late. Everyone will be in bed." The mallard waddled on, looking tired.

Sprout glanced back at the weasel and hurried after the mallard. "How did you know I was in the grave?"

"On my way back from the reservoir I saw the weasel hanging around, which meant there was still a hen alive in the Hole of Death. I know that awful creature!" The mallard shuddered again, his neck feathers trembling. "He's really something—he always hunts the living. And he's big—bigger than any of the other ones. He hunts the living to show how powerful he is. A living hen like you

20

is good prey. He gets what he's after from time to time. You were lucky."

"That's right, I was lucky. It's all thanks to you." Sprout trotted right behind the mallard. Hearing that she was good prey made her feathers stand on end.

"I've never met a hen like you. It's good that you made a racket. The weasel must have been wondering how he could snatch such feisty prey." The mallard laughed gleefully and looked back at the grave.

There was the weasel, still standing there studying them. Sprout quickly averted her eyes, but the mallard was unruffled. "I'm sure you'll meet him again. That one doesn't give up."

"Really?" Sprout sputtered.

"I think you're the first hen to come out of there alive."

"But I was never dead," Sprout murmured.

The mallard continued on his way. They passed under the acacia tree. "Where will you go?" he asked.

Sprout hesitated. "Well . . . I don't have the tiniest desire to go back to the coop."

"You already said that."

"Riiight, I did." Sprout hoped the mallard would help her out. "Um, couldn't you take me with you?"

"Where? Into the barn?" The mallard shook his head. Sprout had put him on the spot. But, perhaps feeling sorry for her, he didn't say no right away. "I'm not from here. But you're a hen, so maybe . . ." The mallard led her to the barn, where the animals slept at night.

21

INTO THE BARN

The old dog was stretched out on the ground with only his rear in his house. His eyes half-closed, he was on his way to dreamland. But when he caught sight of the mallard and a scrawny, soaking-wet chicken missing all her neck feathers, his eyes grew large. "What a terrible smell!" the dog growled, stepping forward.

Sprout sidled closer to the mallard.

"No need to do that. It's just a hen," the mallard said gently so as not to offend the dog.

The dog frowned and circled Sprout, as though waiting for a chance to snatch her up in his jaws. "I can't let just anyone by. I'm an excellent guard!" The dog bared his teeth.

Hearing the commotion, several ducks stuck their heads out of the barn. "So he didn't leave after all?" one duck groused.

"Oh, no," another duck lamented. "What's he dragged in?"

"What a mess! A plucked chicken. It must have run away from the weasel's dinner table."

The ducks quacked with laughter.

The mallard was quiet, but his feathers stood on end and trembled. Sprout felt sorry that he was the butt of their jokes.

"Hey, Straggler!" a duck called. "You're too much of a burden for us as it is. And now you've dragged some sick chicken along with you?"

"Shoo her away! She'll infect us all."

In chorus, the brace of ducks agreed that Sprout should leave immediately.

The dog growled triumphantly, "Got it? Don't you even think about hanging around here."

Sprout was cowed. But she had nowhere else to go. She remained right behind Straggler. "I won't get anyone sick. I won't bother anyone," she said, sniffling. The yard animals weren't strangers to her—she had thought everything would work out if she just left the coop. "And I've wanted to live in the yard for a long time."

"What? You're an egg-laying hen. You need to lay eggs in the coop!" the dog thundered.

"But I . . ." Sprout stammered, trying to stand her ground.

The dog grew more ferocious, lunging at her with his nostrils flaring until she fell on her bottom. This happened several times. The ducks laughed riotously. Sprout burst into tears.

"You're being cowards! Just leave the hen alone!" Straggler shouted at them. "I came here to ask everyone's opinion. How could you be so cruel?"

"Cruel? Does he forget who let him live in the shed?" one of the ducks grumbled.

Straggler grew even more indignant. "This hen escaped

from the Hole of Death! No other hen has come out of there alive. The weasel had his eye on her, but she escaped. She's brave!"

The ducks looked surprised.

"She stood up to the weasel!" he continued. "Could any of you do that? You would have met your end as you tried to waddle away."

The ducks grew silent in the face of Straggler's vigorous defense. The old dog stopped growling.

"What's the big deal? We can just give her a corner of the barn," Straggler proposed.

Sprout marveled at his confidence. Because he always brought up the rear when the ducks went somewhere, she had always thought of him as a duckling.

"Be quiet!" scolded another duck, the leader of the brace, emerging from the barn. "You're an outsider. How dare you insult us? Don't forget we let you live in the barn. You should be grateful!"

The rooster came out to see what the ruckus was about. "I am the head of the barn! Straggler has no right to say this or that. I make every decision!" Everyone deferred to the rooster. His voice was commanding, just as it was when he crowed at dawn. The rooster continued: "Don't you make a fuss. It's late, so the weasel might come by. The hen can stay in the barn. But only tonight. The coop's closed anyway. She can sleep on the outer edge. And as soon as I announce the dawn, she must leave at once!"

The rooster went back into the barn. The leader of the

ducks followed, as did the mallard. Cautiously Sprout went in last. The old, cantankerous dog paced the yard.

The barn was cozy. Bowls of water and feed were spread out, and a warm tangle of hay sat in one corner. There was no wire mesh like the one that had constrained Sprout each time she tried to flap her wings. The rooster and his hen fluttered up to the roost and looked down at everyone. The ducks huddled together. Straggler crouched near the door, some distance away. That seemed to be his spot. Sprout knew she had to be even farther away from the group. So she settled on the outer edge of the barn and didn't dare dream of nestling in the warm hay.

"I can't believe this has happened again," grumbled the hen in the roost. "That hen has to leave in the morning. I'm very sensitive these days. I'm about to lay eggs. If I'm to hatch chicks, everything must be peaceful. I'm sure everyone remembers that I've lost all my chicks!"

Sprout looked up at the hen in the roost. Even in the dark she could appreciate her beauty—her voluptuous body, lustrous feathers, and neat comb. She was a lovely companion to the gallant rooster. Sprout was envious. She wondered if she had ever been that elegant. *And she's going to hatch an egg! I want to know what that's like. I wish I could be just like her.* Sprout had never paid attention to the way she looked. But she knew she was particularly unattractive right now—bedraggled and featherless. Suddenly ashamed, she huddled into herself and blinked back tears. She didn't want anyone staring at her bare neck. To console herself, she remembered that she had escaped the coop and was with the yard animals now. *Soon I'll be able to lay an egg. Soon enough!* But then she remembered her departure orders. Her future looked bleak. And she was starving.

Still, Sprout slept well for the first time in a long while. She was the first to wake, even earlier than the rooster, but she didn't move. She wanted to revel in the coziness of the barn, and she didn't want to disturb the sleeping animals. She grew hopeful. *Maybe they'll let me stay. The mallard is a straggler, and he's settled here. They'll understand if they know how much I want to live in the yard.*

The rooster got up. He smoothed his feathers and stretched his wings, then lengthened his neck and shouted, "Cock-a-doodle-doo!" He fluttered down from the roost near Sprout. She sprang up to let him by.

"I'll give you until I flap my wings and crow on top of the rock wall. Then you must be gone," the rooster ordered. "We let the mallard stay because he really doesn't have a place to go. But you have your own place. The coop. It's safe there. No matter how brave a hen you are, you can't keep running from the weasel." He puffed up with pride. "I gave you a place to sleep last night because you're our kind. But our kind can't become the laughingstock of the barn. Now you have to go back to where you belong."

"I don't want to go back. I want to live in the yard. I won't need to worry about the weasel here," Sprout pleaded. "I was culled."

"Culled?" Sprout nodded, and the rooster laughed derisively. He glared at her, as though he would peck her if she responded. "Nobody wants you!"

Sprout's hopes were dashed. Humiliated, she set her beak firmly. The rooster went out. A moment later she heard his crow, her signal to leave. She glanced at the mallard, who was awake and watching her. But Straggler couldn't help—he was at the bottom of the pecking order. He gave her an apologetic look. Sprout understood. He had done all he could, helping her when she was about to be the weasel's dinner and standing up for her when the yard animals refused her. Sprout left the barn, but she didn't have anywhere to go. She crouched under the acacia tree. The farmer pushed the wheelbarrow toward the coop. When she was in the coop, Sprout would eagerly await the moment the door opened to get a glimpse of the yard she never thought she would reach. Yet here she was! *I shouldn't be sad. It's a miracle that I'm here at all!* Sprout looked up at the acacia tree, which reached toward the sky. *I'm going to lay an egg. And I'm going to hatch a chick. If I survived the weasel, then nothing can stop me!* Her stomach rumbled. Sprout salivated as she watched the farmer's wife feed the yard animals. She wanted to eat, too. She stood up and ran toward a trough. She had no idea where she got the energy. Before she could reach it, a duck bit her mercilessly on the neck. "How dare you?"

Without any feathers to protect her neck, Sprout nearly fainted from the pain.

"Get lost! Now!" snapped the duck before shoving his head in the trough. The other ducks surrounded it, their tails pointing to the sky. There was nowhere for Sprout to wedge herself in.

Sprout glanced at the rooster couple's trough. There was enough room there, but she knew she couldn't. The rooster was greedy and ferocious. And she didn't dare think about approaching the dog.

The farmer looked at Sprout as he pushed the wheelbarrow out of the coop. His wife, on her way inside to retrieve eggs, stopped next to him. "Somehow survived," she said.

Her husband nodded. "It's a tough one."

"Should I put it back in the coop? Oh, right, this one can't lay eggs. Should we eat it?"

Sprout was petrified. But the farmer shook his head. "It's sick anyway. It'll die eventually. Or a weasel will get to it."

Sprout breathed a sigh of relief. But she wished she could eat something, anything. She tried swallowing air. The hens in the coop would be busy eating right now. Her empty intestines felt knotted up. Although life in the yard was more difficult than she had imagined, she didn't even glance at the coop. The compost pile! She remembered the rooster couple digging in it. Sprout headed there without a clue as to what she might find. She was pleased to see a juicy worm wriggling in the dirt. It looked perfectly delicious. The rooster's hen ran over. "Don't you eat my snack!" She gave Sprout a sharp peck on the head. Sprout screamed and backed away. Unappeased, the hen pecked Sprout all over and herded her off the yard. Sprout's entire body ached. But her hunger trumped her pain. She decided to go to the garden. She pecked bits of dewy green cabbage, a lovely relief from both hunger and thirst. Afraid the rooster and hen would run over to guard their territory, Sprout kept exploring. The garden wasn't the only source of food; vast fields surrounded her. Sprout stood tall and proud, clucking joyfully. The rooster and the hen couldn't rule over all this!

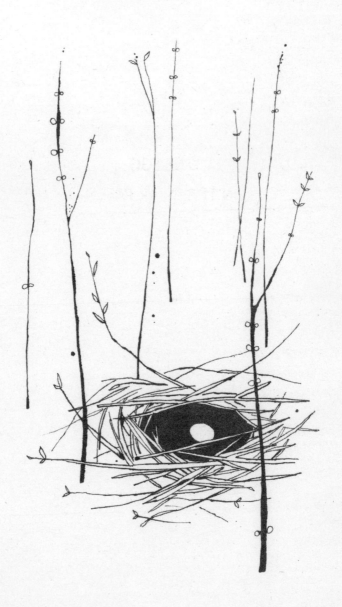

THE EGG
IN THE BRIAR PATCH

Sprout spent the entire day in the fields. She snacked on caterpillars, scratched at the dirt, and took a refreshing snooze on her stomach. There was so much more to do than she had imagined. Nobody bothered her—the ducks went over the hill and didn't return all day, and the rooster couple didn't venture beyond the garden. Sprout was content. But as dusk fell she began to worry. She had to find a safe place away from the weasel. She looked around the fields for a secluded spot to sleep. But there was nowhere she could hide. So she went back to the yard.

The yard animals had already retired to the barn, and the old dog was standing guard. When he spotted Sprout he came over with an unwelcoming expression. "No dice today. Nobody's going to take your side." He circled her several times. "Straggler was warned. If he causes trouble he has to leave the barn. So he won't help you anymore."

Sprout warily hunched her shoulders.

The dog continued: "And it's time for the hen to lay her eggs. I have a duty to keep everything peaceful for her. I don't want you hanging around here." Sprout could tell he was fearful of the hen's bad temper. If the hen got angry at him, she would peck him on the snout—he didn't want to be bossed around by a chicken.

"I don't have anywhere else to sleep," Sprout said politely. She wasn't trying to get into the barn like the night before; she just hoped to sleep under the dog's protection. She didn't care where she slept, as long as it was in the yard.

"That's not my problem. I'm going to get busier and busier. The hen wants to sit on her eggs in a quiet place. Right over there." He gestured to a thicket of bamboo near the pile of compost. It seemed like the kind of place the weasel might raid at night. "Soon enough I'm going to have to patrol that area, too. At my age! The hen is depending on me. If she knows you're hanging around, she's going to get crabby. I'm too old to deal with that." He sighed.

"I won't make a peep. Just let me stay a little while. Under the stone wall or at the edge of the yard. I'll get up before the rooster and leave."

"You're asking too much. All my life I've been a strict gatekeeper. I can't break the rules for you."

"Why can't I live in the yard? I'm a hen, too, just like she is."

"Ha! Silly chicken. What makes you think that? Yes, you're both hens, but you're different. How do you not know that? Just like I'm a gatekeeper and the rooster announces the morning, you're supposed to lay eggs in a cage. Not in the yard! Those are the rules."

"What if I don't like the rules? What happens then?"

"Don't be ridiculous!" The dog snorted. He turned around and went into his house, shaking his head. He wouldn't help her. If she annoyed him further she was asking for humiliation—just like she had when the rooster told her, "Nobody wants you."

She left the yard. But she still had nowhere to go. She went to the edge of the yard and started to scratch under the acacia tree until she created a shallow hole. Her claws ached. She would nestle her lower abdomen into the hole. The dog just watched. Sprout's heart was filled with sadness and rage.

Not long after that, the hen began to spend all her days sitting on a nest in the bamboo thicket. Sometimes she visited the compost pile to hunt for bugs, but she no longer went into the garden. Sprout's mood sank. She didn't know how long it had been since she'd laid an egg. She hadn't felt like laying one in the coop, but now she was healthy again, and all the feathers on her neck had grown back. No matter how desperately she wanted an egg, though, she sensed she couldn't lay one. How proud and happy she would be if she only could. Sprout was frustrated. Wandering through the fields to look for fresh food wasn't all that different from life behind bars. She tried to banish these dark thoughts. *Of course I'm going to lay an egg!* She figured it would come naturally once she made a nest for herself—

she couldn't lay an egg when she slept fitfully every night, worrying about the weasel. But deep down she wondered if that was only an excuse. Sometimes she woke up at night startled by the weasel's eyes glinting in the dark. But each time the dog had smelled the weasel and growled. The weasel had been unable to come near her, and Sprout hadn't had to hurtle into the yard to escape. *If I can't lay an egg, what's the point of my life?*

Sprout felt even more alone because Straggler had found a mate. For quite a while now he never went anywhere without a white duck by his side. The first day she followed the brace of ducks to the reservoir, Sprout saw Straggler playfully splashing the white duck and hopping on her back. Sprout was happy for her friend. But his former loneliness had leached onto her like an infectious disease. Straggler, in turn, changed when he found his best friend. He didn't tag along at the end of the line of ducks, and some nights he didn't come back to the barn. On those nights Sprout couldn't fall asleep, nervous as she was for her friend.

One day, as she was eating breakfast in the fields, Sprout spotted the ducks waddling single file toward the reservoir. Straggler wasn't with them. Sprout watched them disappear around the hill and followed them, hoping to spot the mallard. She thought she would rest easy if she caught a glimpse of him. But he wasn't at the reservoir; nor was the white duck. *Did he leave?* Sprout had thought they were friends. Would he leave without saying good-bye? If she'd known he was going to disappear, she would have said good-bye, even if only in her heart. *I should be the one to leave. I want to leave the yard.* For the first time ever, Sprout found herself missing the coop. At least she was able to lay eggs there. Life wouldn't be so lonely and tedious if she had just behaved like every other hen. She didn't know what to do. She turned to look at the path she'd taken. The yard suddenly seemed so far away. *I don't want to go back to the yard.* It wasn't because of the mallard that she had wanted to live in the yard, but now that he wasn't there she didn't feel like going back. She wanted to escape from the heat and go to sleep for a long time. *Nobody likes me.* She didn't want to live under the acacia tree anymore; she looked longingly at the barn.

She noticed a thick briar patch she'd never paid attention to growing on the skirt of the hill. It would provide good shelter against the heat. A nest didn't have to be in the yard. Sprout was almost upon the briar patch when she heard a piercing scream. Her feathers stood on end. The fields quickly regained their calm, but something ominous scuttled past Sprout's field of vision. Something that looked like a stubby tail blended into a thick cluster of ferns, then disappeared. The ferns rustled a bit, but that was all. Sprout couldn't hear anything else. She stood frozen in place for quite some time, the screech ricocheting in her heart. She felt dizzy and closed her eyes; everything turned red. She opened her eyes cautiously to rid herself of the reddish glaze and looked carefully around her. *Straggler!* She shuddered, just like she had in the Hole of

Death. Even though she knew she had to leave this place immediately, she continued toward the briar patch. Telling herself to stay alert, she put strength into her claws and opened her eyes wide to shore up her courage. *It's okay. Nobody can hurt me.* On she walked, one step at a time. She was convinced it was Straggler who'd screamed. She'd never heard such terror in any animal's voice. But she was prepared to stand her ground, even if she were to come face-to-face with the weasel. If it was her friend in trouble, there was no way she would back down. But she couldn't see a thing. She didn't find even a stray feather, let alone the weasel. All she saw was tall grass and thick branches. She must have imagined it. Feeling relieved, she stuck her head into the briar patch. It was a lovely spot for a nest, surrounded by a thick tumble of ferns. But something was there.

"My goodness, what is that?" Sprout pulled her head out of the patch in confusion and blinked. She shoved her head back in. "How pretty!"

In the middle of the patch was a white egg with a slight bluish cast to it. An egg that hadn't yet been wrapped by feathers. It was large and handsome, but there was no sign of its mother or that it was being incubated. Sprout looked around to see if the mother was nearby. Her heart thumped wildly. *Whose is it? What do I do? What do I do?* Clucking, she paced. She couldn't leave it behind. If she didn't look after it, it might never hatch. Sprout decided to stay just until the mother returned. She entered the briar patch and lay carefully on top of the egg. It was still warm; it had just been laid. *You almost got into trouble, little one. I'll keep you warm. Don't be scared.* Instantly her fear lifted, and peace descended over the briar patch. Joy bubbled up inside her. Closing her eyes, Sprout reveled in the warm mass tucked under her breast. The inside of the briar patch was surprisingly cozy. As evening fell, it became dark more quickly than it did under an oak tree, and the sound of the breeze fell away. "I know I can't lay eggs anymore," Sprout said to herself. "But it's okay. I'm sitting on an egg! My dreams are coming true. It's only one egg, but that's fine with me." She wanted to believe she had rediscovered one of the many long-lost eggs she had laid in the past. But she couldn't help staring into the darkness in case the mother returned. As the buzzing of insects died down, Sprout plucked the feathers off her chest to better feel the egg. A lump hardened in her throat. *This is my egg. My baby that I can tell my stories to!* Already Sprout loved the egg. Even if the mother came back, she wasn't sure she could give it up. She concentrated solely on keeping the egg warm; she could feel the tiny heart beating inside the shell.

Morning dawned. Everything was different from the day before. Sprout covered the egg with the feathers she'd plucked off her chest and emerged from the briar patch. She nibbled on a bit of dew-soaked grass. She couldn't go too far while she was sitting on an egg, so she had to make do with what was nearby. The ducks were waddling along the waterway, headed to the reservoir. The leader was at the front, and the youngest duck took up the rear. Straggler was not with them. Once again Sprout wished she'd had a chance to say good-bye, but she didn't feel as alone as before. She searched around for dry grass that would keep the egg warmer. As she headed back toward the briar patch with some blades of grass in her beak, she heard something behind her. Straggler! She was so stunned that she almost dropped everything. He looked exhausted and sad. She was glad to see him, but she stopped in her tracks so he wouldn't catch her with her egg. He gazed quietly at Sprout's plucked chest before sitting down. Eventually Sprout went back into the briar patch and settled over the egg. She wondered what had happened to her friend. He didn't tell her anything, but from time to time he moved his head out from under his wing and looked at her with sad eyes. Sprout wondered why his expression was so dark. She wondered where the white duck was.

Straggler didn't leave until dawn. She felt for him, but she was grateful he didn't ask her any questions about the egg. As the mist-shrouded sun came up, Straggler headed to the reservoir with the other ducks. A while later he returned, a fish hanging from his bill. He placed it in front of the patch and left again.

A FAREWELL
AND A GREETING

S traggler brought Sprout a fish every day. Thanks to him, she was able to sit on the egg without getting hungry. Why didn't he go back to the barn? Why was he feeding her? Why did he pace around the patch all night? She was curious about everything he did but didn't have a chance to ask. Other than to bring her food, he didn't come near her, and she had to sit on the egg without moving. She whispered to the egg, "Baby, Straggler climbed up the hill and is looking someplace far away. I think he's looking beyond the reservoir."

On nights when the moon was particularly bright, Straggler ran around flapping his wings. This was new— he'd never done that in the yard. The first time she witnessed Straggler waddling around as fast as he could, Sprout told the egg, "Baby, Straggler's right wing doesn't open fully. I wonder what happened. But his left wing is bigger and more powerful than I thought. His wings don't look like the other ducks' wings." On the nights Straggler ran around like that, Sprout told the egg numerous stories. Or she sang lullaby after lullaby in case the egg was startled by Straggler's loud quacks ringing through the hills. Straggler looked like he was dancing, and Sprout couldn't help but be concerned. His behavior was becoming more and more erratic. But she didn't ask him about it. She didn't want to embarrass him, especially when he was so kind to bring her food each day.

As the full moon started to wane, Straggler's dancing became more frequent, and Sprout's worries more pronounced. Sprout had been sitting on the egg since the moon was a crescent; the baby inside was almost all grown, its heartbeat strong. Soon the shell would crack, but Sprout worried the mallard would frighten the baby. A few more days passed. Straggler skipped some nights, but his odd dance continued. Sprout watched patiently.

One night, Straggler kicked up a fuss nonstop. He didn't sleep a wink. He ran about as though he were being chased. It was worse than ever. Sprout, kept awake by the ruckus, decided to have a talk with him. Straggler was a dear friend, but this was really too much. Sprout managed to close her eyes and rest in the morning, when the mallard went to the reservoir. A little later he brought her a fish. Sprout pried open her sleep-laden eyes and shook her head. "Please don't do that again. I wish you wouldn't be so noisy at night."

Straggler didn't answer. He seemed very tired.

"You've been so good to me," Sprout continued. "I'm so grateful. I'll never forget everything you've done for me. But as you know, I'm hatching an egg."

Straggler remained quiet. Sprout must have hurt his feelings. All she did was complain—when he'd saved her from the Hole of Death, when he'd stood up for her so she could stay in the barn, when he'd brought her food. Straggler gazed at the reservoir, deep in thought.

Apologetically, Sprout said, "I'm fine now. My claws are strong and my beak is hard. I won't go down without a fight if the weasel comes back. So you can go and do your own thing."

Straggler looked at her, the feathers on his neck trembling. Sprout shouldn't have mentioned the weasel. "When the egg hatches, maybe when the dark moon . . ." he murmured. Sprout wondered why he was waiting for her egg to hatch, but he didn't explain. Before returning to the reservoir, he said cryptically, "If I could swim just once more with . . ."

That night went by quietly. Sprout carefully considered the waxing and waning of the moon. A crescent moon had filled out into a full moon, and now it was waning each night, soon to become a dark moon. Incubation was taking longer than she thought, but the heartbeat was still strong. Straggler brought her food as always. Sprout wanted to apologize for what she'd said earlier. "I wouldn't mind so much if you just took it down a notch. With your wings spread wide like that, it looks like you're dancing. Like you're flying away, beautiful and free." Sprout opened her wings and shook them in appeasement. But all she did was create dust. Her wings weren't for flying; they were just for show.

"Flying away?" Straggler asked quietly. He looked out sadly over the reservoir and murmured, "If I could fly again . . ."

"Your wings look different from the other ducks'. Although your right wing is a little strange."

"Right, I bet I look silly. My right wing . . ." Straggler was quiet for a long time, watching Sprout peck eagerly at the loach he'd brought. After her meal, Sprout dug at the ground for exercise and bathed herself with dirt. Her itchy body felt much better. "It's almost time for the egg to hatch, right?" Straggler asked gently.

"It must be overdue. It should have hatched already." Sprout enjoyed sitting across from him and chatting.

"Um, so, later, when the egg hatches—you're a hen—" Straggler stammered, nervously tapping the ground with his bill during the pauses.

Sprout was a little exasperated. "You know, I have a name," she confided. "I gave it to myself."

"Really? I've never heard it."

"Because nobody knows it. Will you call me Sprout?"

"Sprout? Like grass and leaves?"

"Right. There's nothing better than a sprout. It stands for doing good."

Straggler pondered Sprout's words. From time to time he used his bill to rub the oil from his tail into his feathers.

"A sprout is the mother of flowers," Sprout explained. "It breathes, stands firm against rain and wind, keeps the sunlight, and rears blindingly white flowers. If it weren't for sprouts, there'd be no trees. A sprout is vital."

"Sprout . . . that's a perfect name for you," Straggler agreed. Sprout was pleased. She knew she should try to understand his nocturnal commotion instead of resenting it. Straggler turned serious. "Even without a name like that, you're a really great hen. I wanted to tell you that."

Sprout felt guilty. She was flustered, wondering what Straggler would think if he knew the truth. He would be shocked and appalled. Unable to look him in the eye, Sprout returned to her nest and settled over the egg. She couldn't do anything about it now. She wasn't going to tell anyone, not even her dear friend. *It's my baby! I'm sitting on it, and I'm going to raise it. Surely that makes it my baby.* She changed the subject abruptly. "What happened to your right wing? And where's the white duck?"

Straggler raised his head. His gentle demeanor changed in a flash. "Don't you dare mention it!"

Sprout was taken aback. She didn't know what she was forbidden to mention. Straggler's neck feathers were bristling, the way they did when he spotted the weasel. He tensed and looked around quickly as though he had forgotten something important. Sprout hadn't meant to make him angry. "I thought you left the barn with her," she said gently. "I know the others don't like you. Even though you lived there you were always a loner. Oh, I mean, what I mean is . . ."

Straggler said nothing.

Sprout tried again. "The white duck is your mate, right? I'm your friend, but I—"

"I told you to stop it!" snapped Straggler, cutting Sprout off. He sprang up and stalked away, fuming, waddling even more than usual. Sprout didn't understand why he was so angry. He soon returned, still fuming. He lowered his voice and said stiffly, "The moon's grown slimmer. That means the egg will hatch soon."

"Right, it's past time."

"Sprout, you're an intelligent hen, so you'll know what to do. I just want to tell you a few things. When the egg hatches, leave this place. And go to the reservoir, not the yard, okay? Don't forget that when the moon is waning, the weasel's stomach is empty." Straggler spoke as though he were going to leave. Was he angry at her? And he was telling her so many things at once. Things she didn't quite understand.

"What do you mean the weasel's stomach is empty?" Sprout asked.

"It should be okay. But I'm telling you just in case. Don't go to the yard, go to the reservoir."

"Why?"

Straggler didn't respond. He paced, glancing around, then climbed the hill and looked far off into the distance. Sprout was tense, uneasy at the mention of the weasel. After coming across the wild briar patch, she had put the weasel out of her mind. She hadn't seen his glinting eyes once while sitting on the egg. If the weasel had found her, she would have been in grave danger, and her baby would have been harmed. It was an awful thought.

Night fell. Sprout couldn't shake the thought of the weasel. Her heart sank each time the night breeze blew through the grass or the moonlit leaves rustled. Straggler was right outside the briar patch with his head tucked under his wing. That made her feel ill at ease. She would be less frightened if he performed his odd little dance.

A thought suddenly occurred to her. Did Straggler create a fuss at night because of the weasel? To scare him away? Sprout was now completely alert, frightened to the bone. Why would he protect her, going to such lengths for just a friend? *I'm not even a fellow duck.* . . . She looked up at the sky. The stars were hazy and the moon was faint, a sign of rain. Suddenly she thought of the Hole of Death.

It had rained that day, too.

Unable to push away her fear, Sprout stood up. She was going to face the weasel bravely. She planned to raise her claws and peck him mercilessly while flapping her wings. She would holler and put up a fight. She peered into the darkness. The weasel might already be there on the other side of the darkness, that hunter with his slitted eyes glaring in this direction, licking his chops, his stomach empty.

"Wake up, Straggler!" Sprout shouted.

Straggler raised his head in surprise. "Did it hatch?"

"No, but it might as day breaks. Judging by how long it's taking, he might be a full-grown rooster!" Sprout laughed out loud on purpose, but she was still afraid. "I'm getting really worried. What if the weasel comes?"

But Straggler didn't seem to share Sprout's anxiety. "Good!" he exclaimed. "As soon as day breaks. This is great!" He shook his feathers to wake himself and looked around cautiously.

Sprout decided to come clean. She felt bad about lying to her friend, who'd looked after her from the beginning. "Straggler, I have something to tell you. I had a wish. I wanted to hatch an egg and see the birth of a chick. That was an impossible dream in the coop. I didn't want to lay any eggs anymore—I thought I would never be able to—"

Straggler interrupted her. "Sprout, you're a wonderful mother hen."

"I'm not fishing for compliments."

"No, it's true. I'm a wild duck who can't fly, and you're an exceptional hen."

"Okay, but ..."

"That's all there is to it. We look different, so we don't understand each other's inner thoughts, but we cherish each other in our own way. I respect you."

Sprout's breath caught in her throat. Sometimes Straggler puzzled her. "Even if we don't understand each other? How?"

"Because I know you're a wonderful mother," Straggler said firmly. Sprout closed her beak. Somehow confessing about the egg didn't seem so important anymore. "I know that weasel," Straggler continued. "He's a born hunter, so we can't defeat him. He's bigger and stronger than any weasel I've ever seen. Even if it's fine now, he's going to get us in the end. We have to finish our work before that happens." Sprout didn't quite understand what he was talking about, yet she knew it was true. Her heart began to pound. Sprout couldn't believe she had spent all this time without thinking about the weasel. Straggler moved away from the briar patch and murmured, "I hope the egg hatches tomorrow, before it's too late. I'm too tired. The weasel won't be able to hold out any longer." Sprout studied him silently. She didn't know what was between him and the weasel, and that made her even more nervous. Straggler kept talking. "I'm okay. If he's full he'll be quiet for a while. It's okay, as long as the egg hatches. I'm ready."

Sprout could no longer hear her friend. Straggler settled away from his usual spot and buried his head under his wing to sleep. Sprout's feathers stood on end, just as the mallard's had at the mention of the weasel. She turned the egg. With Straggler here nothing would happen, and morning would soon come. Everything was quiet. Even the blades of grass were silent, not rustling against one another. Sprout started to get drowsy. She closed her eyes for a brief moment.

"Quaaaack!"

Sprout's eyes flew open. Straggler! His short, horrifying scream echoed in her heart. In the moonless dark, the mallard was flapping with all his might. Some creature was gripping his writhing, dark body. There were no longer any screams. Straggler's neck must have been broken. Sprout shuddered, and her throat closed up. "Straggler!" She sprang up and ran outside, her eyes glaring and her wings flapping. The weasel, with the mallard in his mouth, shot her a chilling look. Sprout's heart turned to ice. The weasel's flashing eyes warned her not to approach. Sprout hesitated. She couldn't win with only her claws and beak. Trembling, she watched the tragic end of her friend as his limp body was dragged away. The weasel disappeared into the darkness; the forest and the fields became quiet all too quickly. Although a precious life was snuffed out in an instant, the world was serene. The trees, stars, moon, and grass were hushed as though they'd witnessed nothing. Sprout ran off after the weasel. But there was only darkness; there was no trace of him. Wanting to find something, anything, even a feather, Sprout searched all over the dark hill. She couldn't stop weeping. Straggler was dead. And she'd done nothing to help him. She had been stupidly scared. He had died alone. The weasel's eyes had chilled her to the bone. From the moment Sprout had left the coop, the weasel's eyes had always followed her. Straggler had shielded her from the realization that the briar patch wasn't safe. He had stayed awake every night to guard her and her egg from the weasel. *Why didn't you stay awake tonight? Why didn't you cry out a warning? Poor thing!* He must have been exhausted. Sprout shivered. She could have been the one to die. Everything would have ended in an instant.

Morning dawned. The sun began to rise from beyond the reservoir, dampened by fog as usual, illuminating the spot where Straggler usually sat. He who would watch the sun and shake out his feathers was no longer. Sprout vowed never to forget him. She flapped her wings at the sun, in farewell to her friend. *Oh!* The egg had been alone for a long time by now. Sprout rushed into the briar patch. She couldn't believe her eyes.

A baby was tottering out!

It had cracked the shell on its own. This amazing, downy creature looked at Sprout, its black eyes shining.

"Oh, my goodness!" Sprout stood still, in a daze. She had known there was a baby inside the egg, but this was like a dream. Small eyes, small wings, small feet—everything was tiny. But they all moved, and every movement was tiny and adorable. "Baby, you're here!" Sprout ran over and embraced him with outstretched wings. He was a real baby, all small and warm. She could hear the ducks going to the reservoir. Outside, it seemed nothing had changed since the day before, but for her it was a special morning. In various parts of the fields things happened without interruption. Someone died, and someone was born. Sometimes a farewell and a greeting happened at the same time. Sprout knew she couldn't be sad for long.

A DISGRACE
TO THE COMB

Sprout marched confidently toward the barnyard with her fuzzy light brown baby in tow. Straggler's suggestion that she leave the nest once the egg hatched hadn't been a flippant comment. He was protecting her baby from the weasel. She had to take Baby to safety before the weasel's stomach—currently full on her mallard friend—grew empty again. The dog, who had been dozing in the midday heat, was the first to spot Sprout. "Look who's here!" he barked. The rooster's hen ran over from the stone wall, where she had been digging. Six yellow chicks tagged along. The chicks had immaculate yellow fur without a single light brown tuft. "Who is that?" the hen asked, frowning. She clucked for the rooster to come out. The rooster, not a fan of the strong sun, took his sweet time.

Sprout stopped under the shade of the acacia tree and waited for Baby to catch up. He was traveling too far too soon after being born. He tripped and fell several times on the way, but he managed to make it to the yard with tottering steps. The dog sniffed at Baby and circled him, setting Sprout on edge. The hen clucked, and the chicks kept up a steady chatter of cheeps. Then the hen groused, "How could she possibly hatch an egg? It doesn't make any sense."

The chicks, who were learning to talk, rang out after her in chorus, "How could she possibly hatch an egg? It doesn't make any sense!"

"Shush! You don't have to learn that."

"Shush! You don't have to learn that."

"My goodness, I can't say anything."

The chicks began, "My goodness," when the hen quickly said, "It's tasty snack time!" and ran toward the compost pile.

"It's tasty snack time!" The six chicks ran after her.

Sprout watched the chicks with a smile. They were very cute. Their yellow fur was especially pretty. Having never seen a chick up close, Sprout assumed her baby's light brown fur would turn yellow in time. She settled under the acacia tree and tucked Baby under her wing. No matter what anyone said, she wouldn't leave the yard until he was fully grown. Humiliation would surely follow, but that was better than being eaten by the weasel.

"What a mess!" barked the dog, raising his head.

Unable to ignore the ruckus, the rooster finally came out of the barn. He was shocked to see Sprout. Perhaps in disbelief that she was still alive, he paced the yard with his eyes glued to her. The dog whispered something to the rooster, who glared at Sprout. "Is that right? Let me see the baby." Sprout was scared, but she remained where she was. She didn't want to do what the rooster demanded. "Let me see that duckling, I said!" thundered the rooster, his neck feathers standing on end.

Sprout was taken aback. Duckling? The hen ran over, and the chicks surrounded Sprout. Sprout stayed where she was, Baby still tucked under her wing. Past events flitted through her head. The egg in the briar patch, Straggler, the fish, the scream, the light brown feathers . . . *a duckling?* All her baby's toes *were* welded together. His beak was round and he waddled, but she had chalked it all up to his youth. The world started spinning, the way it had spun her first day out when she poked her beak in the trough and was bitten by a duck. Now it all made sense. The first time she went to the briar patch, she'd heard a scream. She'd thought it was the mallard, but maybe it had been the white duck! That was why the egg was there and why Straggler came. *I was incubating the white duck's egg. Straggler knew everything—when the egg would hatch and that he had to die so it could live.* That final night when the exhausted mallard had fallen asleep, he was quietly giving up his life, knowing the egg would soon hatch. He had hoped Sprout and Baby would leave the nest while the weasel was full. That was why he told her to go to the reservoir, not the yard. Sprout's throat closed up, and her body stiffened. Pain seared her heart like on that awful day she'd laid a soft wrinkly egg. *Straggler, you were a wonderful father! What should I do now?*

Baby poked his head out from under Sprout's wing. Sprout was flustered, but she let him; she couldn't keep him in hiding. He came out and joined the chicks. Even though he was light brown and the others were yellow, the babies played happily together. *Poor thing! He must think he's a chick, too.*

"See? I told you!" barked the dog, triumphant.

The rooster glared at Sprout as the hen jeered, "A culled chicken couldn't have laid an egg! How indecent. If you were sold to a restaurant, then you wouldn't be such a disgrace!"

Sprout stared at the hen in confusion.

The rooster explained sternly, "She means it's more dignified to become a dish at a restaurant. Aren't you ashamed? You, a member of the comb, hatched a baby of another kind!"

"I'll say," the dog taunted. "A chicken hatching a duck! What a ridiculous sight!"

The rooster, whose bad mood was getting worse, ran over to peck at the dog, who inched away and retreated into his house. The rooster's feathers stood on end. "It's a disgrace to the comb!" he grumbled. "A ridiculous hen has made our kind the laughingstock of the barn. How dare they laugh at us, the voice of the sun, the possessor of the comb! Foolish hen!" The rooster paced the yard, agonizing, frowning, and sometimes stopping to glare at Sprout. "This cannot stand!" the rooster announced with finality.

Sprout's thoughts were jumbled, but she was anything

but ashamed. She had hatched her egg with all her being. She had wished for him to be born. She'd loved him from when he was inside the egg. She was never suspicious about what was inside. *Sure, he's a duck, not a chick. Who cares? He still knows I'm his mom!*

Night fell. When the ducks returned from the reservoir, the rooster held a meeting to discuss "the problem of the foolish hen and the duckling." The rooster wanted to get rid of Sprout and the duckling immediately, but he'd overheard the owners speaking to each other:

"Look at that hen," the farmer's wife had remarked. "Nice and plump! Where did she come from?"

The farmer was pleased. "And a free duckling! We should put them in the barn."

Despite the rooster's objections, Sprout and Baby seemed destined to live in the barn. The disgruntled rooster presided over the meeting. As the leader of the barn, he had to save face before accepting Sprout and the duckling. The rooster went up to the roost to look down at everyone; the hen snuggled in the haystack with her chicks. The ducks clustered around their leader, and Sprout held Baby in her wings and sat with her back to the door. As the gatekeeper, the dog kept only his front legs in the barn as he listened to the rooster.

"As you all know, this is a complicated problem," the rooster announced, shooting Sprout a derisive look. "This chicken hatched a duck egg and came to live in the yard. As the head of the barn I can make a unilateral decision. But I want to hear what the ducks have to say because it's a problem for both the chickens and the ducks. What should we do with this foolish chicken? And what should we do with that duckling?"

The hen spoke up first. "One hen in the barn is enough. And I have six chicks. There isn't room. I'm also worried about the chicks' education. I know they'll keep asking, 'Why does he quack and call a hen Mom?' 'Why is he different from us?' Some of them might even try to quack. I can't raise my chicks in a chaotic environment like that. We need to send the foolish hen and the duckling packing."

"That's right," the dog chimed in. "Keeping order is first and foremost!"

Sprout tightened her embrace of her duckling, who was squirming to get out from under her wings. The yard animals might become incensed if Baby pranced around in their faces, and this discussion had to go well.

"Well," said the leader of the ducks in a gracious voice, "the duckling is young. If we send him out like this, he'll surely die. So we should let them stay. The duckling is our kind, so I think my opinion takes precedence. Straggler and the white duck were killed by the weasel. We don't have enough in our family. And I don't know how long it's been since I've seen such a young baby. As you are all aware, we can't hatch any eggs these days."

"That's ridiculous," scoffed the hen. "You don't have enough in your family? How can you say that when the entire barn is filled with ducks? And that one doesn't even know he's a duckling."

The leader of the ducks didn't back down. "That can be taught. A hen hatched him, but he's still a duck. He has to swim and fish. I'll teach him myself. We can't send him off. That's our decision."

"We have to!" the hen shot back, flapping her wings. "If we take in every stray, next time it might even be the weasel asking to settle down in the barn. This is exactly how it all starts!"

The dog grumbled unhappily, "Watch it! You're insulting the best gatekeeper!"

The ducks began quacking all at once. The hen clucked on without pausing for breath. The debate didn't end until the night was deep; it grew so noisy that the farmer and his wife came to the barn with flashlights to investigate.

"Turf war. I'm going to have to do something in the morning," the farmer said, pointing his flashlight into the corners to illuminate the upended water bowl and feathers floating in the air. The animals quieted down, and the flashlight stopped on Sprout. "Now look at that!" The farmer was pleased.

"Not bad, right?" his wife asked, and they headed out of the barn.

Concerned about their conversation, Sprout kept listening, wondering what they had planned for the morning.

"Should I put it in the coop?" the farmer's wife wondered. "Or we can boil it for soup tomorrow evening."

"Whatever you want," the farmer said. "By the way, I think that duckling is wild. Shouldn't we put him in a cage or clip his wings?"

Sprout was taken aback. But she was the only one who heard the couple's conversation. Once again the rooster and the hen were arguing with the ducks. Even the dog was getting riled up.

"We have to send him away!" the hen clucked.

"Never!" quacked the ducks.

"Not once have I let you down as gatekeeper!" barked the dog.

Sprout was still focused on the farmer and his wife's plans. She could end up back in the coop, or as soup. She couldn't stop trembling. Learning that was as frightening as seeing the weasel's eyes. She regretted returning to the yard. Was this why Straggler had told her to go to the reservoir instead? Surreptitiously she wiped her eyes. She had to leave the yard immediately, before she was shut in the coop and Baby's wings were clipped. That night passed slowly. Sprout didn't let herself fall asleep because she knew they had to leave before everyone woke up.

The sun appeared on the horizon. Sprout could faintly make out the trees in the hills. Usually the rooster would have woken up by now, but because he had gone to bed so late his eyes were still closed. The dog, too, was sound asleep.

Sprout whispered to the duckling under her wing. "Baby, let's leave. Quietly."

"Okay, Mom."

Sprout got up quietly and tiptoed out. The duckling followed stealthily. The yard remained shrouded in the bluish darkness of dawn. Sprout wasn't worried, though, as it would soon be daylight. She crossed the yard toward the acacia tree and then looked back sadly. She would never return. Looking straight ahead, stiffening her claws, setting her beak firmly, and with fierce eyes, she walked resolutely into the twilight.

CERTAINLY A DUCK

The road to the reservoir was rugged. It marked the beginning of their wretched life as wanderers in the fields without the protection of the gatekeeper or the barn, the weasel always on their minds. Sprout asked Straggler to give her courage. She had to protect Baby until he was grown. She'd always talked to herself, but now she could talk to the mallard, who remained in her heart.

Baby grew tired before they reached the reservoir; they had to rest. Sprout led him to a rice paddy. They drank from the irrigation ditch and caught grasshoppers between rice stalks to fill their bellies. Baby soon fell asleep under the shade of curly docks. Sprout, who had spent the previous night with her eyes wide-open, fell into a sweet, irresistible slumber.

"What is this?" A loud quacking assaulted her ears, but Sprout couldn't open her eyes. Her eyelids felt heavy, as if they had been welded together. "You have no idea how dangerous this is!" someone scolded.

"My goodness, what was I thinking?" Sprout jumped to her feet.

The leader of the ducks was looking down at them from the top of the hill. The other ducks were behind him. "Why did you run away? You'd be safer in the barn."

"Well, I just . . ." Sprout hesitated. Maybe she shouldn't tell him the yard wasn't safe for them. What good would it do to tell him that she'd figured out the farmer and his wife's plans? "I felt bad that you were fighting because of us. We're going to the reservoir."

Sprout climbed up the hill with her duckling and started toward the reservoir again. The ducks crowded around Baby. The female ducks in particular couldn't tear themselves away from the adorable duckling, but Baby followed only Sprout.

"Thank you for hatching the egg," one of the ducks said to Sprout. "He's the cutest ever! Our eggs are sold or go to the incubator, so none of us has had the experience of having a baby. What a blessing that there's a baby in the family!"

Sprout stopped. "Family?" she snapped. "I don't plan on giving you the baby."

"What? What do you think you're going to do with him? You're a hen."

"I'm his mom. They'll clip his wings. You think I'm going to let him go back to the barnyard?"

"That's why you ran away? Don't be scared. It doesn't hurt at all. It just stings a little. He might not even feel it. So he won't fly away."

"So he won't fly away?"

"This baby looks more like a wild duck than one of us. If you don't domesticate him, he'll be in danger. He'll forever be a wanderer like Straggler and end up killed."

Sprout continued on silently. Straggler's end was tragic, but she wouldn't even consider giving Baby away.

The leader followed her and persisted in trying to convince her. "Think about Straggler. He was always alone. It's hard to live in between, as neither wild nor domesticated. He couldn't change his fate. He lost his mate to the weasel and wounded his wing. He couldn't fly, so he couldn't return to the winterlands."

"The weasel hurt his wing?"

"Who else?"

Sprout nodded in silence. Now she understood why his neck feathers would tremble at the mere mention of the weasel.

"He found a mate in the white duck, but she was done in by the weasel, too." The leader sighed. "All because he couldn't change his wild duck ways. If the white duck had hatched the egg in the barn, she would still be with us. Well, I guess if the farmer took it, she wouldn't have been able to hatch it!"

Sprout shuddered, that final night coming to her in a flash. Now she knew what Straggler had been thinking. They had been harboring the same wish. If she had only realized it earlier! He had been nervous the entire time, worried she wouldn't sit on the egg if she knew it was a duck's. But she wouldn't have refused even if she'd known. Nobody could possibly know how happy she'd been when she sat on the egg. Sprout slowed down to match Baby's gait. The female ducks fell back unwillingly. Sprout felt surging hatred toward the weasel. He'd taken every precious being. She wanted to be stronger than the weasel to get revenge. But she knew it was foolish. Revenge? Just thinking about living in the wide-open fields again was enough to make her cry. But she held her tears at bay and set her beak.

They arrived at the reservoir. The ducks jumped in, clamoring to be the first to get in. But the leader and Baby remained next to Sprout.

"Look at this. He doesn't know that he's a duck or that he can swim. Even though his feet are webbed, he probably thinks he's a chick!" The leader, wings outstretched, tried to herd Baby into the water. Baby resisted, screaming.

"Leave him alone!" Sprout shot at him angrily, her feathers bristling. Baby scampered under her wings.

The leader sighed. "This is wrong. Even though a hen hatched him, he's still a duck." He shook his head and swam toward his ducks.

Sprout's heart was heavy. But she had to find a nest. She strolled along the edge of the water away from the clamor of the ducks. She didn't know what to do. All she knew was that she had to stay alert so they didn't fall victim to the weasel. A thatch of reeds appeared. Sprout fell for the place at first glance. Dried reeds were strewn on the ground, and new reeds were clustered together, creating a most excellent hiding place. It was beautiful there, with blooming water lilies and water hyacinths, but the best part was the abundance of food. This area was teeming with throaty frogs perched on lily pads, dragonflies resting on reed stalks, small fish that came to the surface of the water, locusts, and diving beetles. It would make a great home. *I hope nobody finds us.* Sprout constructed a nest of dried reed leaves. Only a small bird would be able to weave through the dense water plants.

Baby hopped on a lily pad.

"Baby, careful!"

"Careful, careful!" He quacked happily before leaping onto another pad. It made Sprout nervous, but she couldn't hold him back. Baby hopped from pad to pad until he was in the middle of the reservoir.

"Baby, come back!"

"Mom, look where I am!" He waved his little wing joyously. The lily pad tipped, and he fell into the water.

"Baby!" Sprout panicked. Surprised, Baby flailed about. Sprout ran into the reservoir, but her feathers became waterlogged, and she barely managed to get out.

"Mom, look at me!" the duckling called out, short of breath, floundering.

Sprout looked closely—Baby wasn't drowning; he was definitely swimming, albeit clumsily. Dripping wet, Sprout laughed loudly. Her baby was doing things he hadn't been taught. "Yes, you're certainly a duck!"

Days passed peacefully. Sprout lost weight to better navigate through the reeds. She made sure to be quiet so she wouldn't alarm their neighbors. A pair of reed warblers had built a nest nearby and laid eggs. The moon filled out, and nobody peeked in the reed thicket. Sprout felt ill at ease whenever she noticed blades of grass casting shadows under the moonlight or reeds rustling in the wind, but she and her baby were safe. Baby was growing every day, and getting better at swimming, diving, and catching fish. Each evening he liked to settle under Sprout's wing to sleep.

One day Baby swam out far and returned with the leader of the ducks. Or, judging from Baby's slightly scared expression, the leader had followed him uninvited. Under orders from the leader, the other ducks kept back a short distance. They played among the water lilies, chattering loudly. Sprout was displeased. The female reed warbler cheeped nervously, and the male flew up several times to see what was going on.

Sprout shook her head. The silly ducks had never incubated an egg, so they didn't have any idea how a mother would feel threatened by their ruckus. She hoped the weasel wouldn't be drawn to the noise and discover their hiding spot. The leader, who was oblivious to her worries, made idle chatter. "He's grown so big I hardly recognize him. He's gotten the best parts of the white duck and Straggler. It's amazing he's figured everything out on his own! Good for him!" The leader tried to stroke Baby, who slipped away and looked first at Sprout, then at the leader. The leader continued: "Even though a hen hatched him, a duck is a duck! Our kind never forgets how to swim or dive. He knows how to do it without being taught. It's not something a chicken, who is confident in the yard but afraid of the fields, can do!"

Sprout snorted at the leader for bragging like he was Baby's father. He didn't know Baby. Baby wouldn't leave her just because the leader praised him. He would never leave her. She puffed her chest out confidently. "Chickens fear the fields?"

"Oh, not you, of course. But the other chickens don't know a thing. I'm sure they don't even know that their ancestors paraded around the skies, like birds."

"Chickens? Like birds?" Sprout couldn't believe her ears. Flying with these wings that only scattered dust? She had seen the rooster jump down from the stone wall with his wings outstretched, but that couldn't be called flying. At the very least, flying required floating up higher than a tree and traveling elsewhere, managing to be afloat for a long time. It would be wonderful if she could fly. "But what happened? Why can't we fly anymore?" Sprout stretched her wings. She wouldn't be able to clear even the tops of the reeds.

"Well, that's because all you do is eat all day and lay eggs," the leader explained. "Your wings grow weaker and your behind grows bigger. And yet you still think you're so great, saying you represent the voice of the sun."

Sprout thought it was laughable that he was bad-mouthing chickens behind the rooster's back; he wouldn't say a word of this to the rooster's face. "So if our behinds grew larger, why was it the ducks that ended up waddling?" Sprout asked gently. "And you have wings, too. What do you use them for?"

The leader coughed and changed the subject. "Actually, I came to talk to you about the duckling. It's dangerous for him to live like this. Let's go back to the barn. Let him, at least, even if you don't want to."

"Nothing bad has happened to us here. If you continue to make such a ruckus, everyone's going to find out where we're hiding. Please go home with your family. We're not going back."

"Two chicks from the barnyard were taken!" the leader pressed. "Because curiosity led them up the hill from behind the garden. The hen is depressed and won't even come out of the barn."

Sprout shook her neck feathers in fright. She didn't understand why the weasel insisted on devouring the living. "Baby, come," she said, wanting to keep her baby safe under her wings. But Baby just looked at her and then at the leader, hurting her feelings a little.

"It was too much for the hen to look after all those chicks by herself," continued the leader. "But we're different. We have a big family, so it'll be easy to look after one duckling. Don't make your life difficult. Let us help. It's inevitable that the weasel will try to take all the chicks now that he's had a taste of tender flesh. You know who's next."

Sprout tensed her claws. She could sense the shadow of the frightening hunter approaching. The weasel would be here soon enough. He might already be looking this way. She glared at the leader, rendering him mute. "Leave us and go. Now," she ordered.

"You're so stubborn! You can't keep thinking of him as a chick. Even though a hen hatched him, a duck is a duck!" the leader said in a huff and then left.

The other ducks raised a fuss when they learned the duckling wasn't coming with them. The reed warblers twittered nervously until the quacking died down. Baby sat in the nest, looking at the retreating ducks. He didn't look as carefree as before. The ducks' ruckus must have bothered him.

"Baby, we need to leave," Sprout said. "It's not safe here anymore."

"Why not?"

"If the ducks found us, the weasel will, too. The weasel is powerful. He can easily hurt us. He hunts the living, and he never gives up. So let's find another nest before nightfall." Sprout gathered their feathers that had scattered on the ground and tossed them in the water. She clawed at the nest and smoothed it over with her wings. Quietly she led the way out of the reed fields to keep from disturbing the reed warblers. The duckling kept looking back, reluctant to leave the water behind. His foot-dragging told Sprout they wouldn't get far.

The day was waning. Sprout climbed a shallow slope of grass that overlooked the reed fields. The cow that had been tied to the willow tree during the day had been led home. It had pulled the rope to its full length in order to graze on the grass at some distance from the tree, so the patch of grass just under the tree was lush and uneaten. Cow patties were scattered around the tree. It would be too dangerous to spend the night in the fields without cover. But Sprout mustered her courage. "I think we can spend one night here. The cow patties will hide our scent." She dug a hole and spent the night in it, her wings wrapped around Baby. The overgrown grass hid them somewhat, but she remained wide awake.

The moon was bright. Baby, who had been quiet all evening, fell asleep, and Sprout could hear only the breeze rustling the grass. Watchful and alert, Sprout looked into the darkness. She was like Straggler now. Back then she'd slept worry-free like Baby, while Straggler had stayed awake to keep the weasel away, flapping his wings and hollering. She had to be brave like Straggler: before he gave up his life, even the weasel was no match for him. She was startled by a memory, as though a drop of cold water had fallen on her head—the weasel hadn't been able to get her in the Hole of Death because she was too feisty. She could face him as long as she was brave. *He can't touch us!*

Sprout stepped away from the hole and looked down at the reed patch. She wished they hadn't had to leave the nest. She was now a wanderer without a home. She hadn't wanted to be shut in a cage, and she couldn't stay in the yard as she'd hoped. She'd had to abandon their nest in the reeds. Tomorrow morning they would leave again. Why was this her life? Was it because she held out hope? She thought about Straggler. He was always in her heart, but often she wished he was right beside her. If she could only hear his voice and see his face—

Sprout caught sight of something moving.

She flattened herself on the ground. A dark shadow swiftly approached the reed fields. The weasel. *I knew it!* She froze in place and began to tremble. The weasel entered the reed fields. The stalks appeared to rustle for a moment, but then she couldn't see anything. Knowing the weasel would come out empty-jawed, she couldn't help but smile. She had won this battle. *We're not there! You can't catch us!* The weasel emerged from the reed fields and ran back to where he had come from.

The next day Sprout and Baby returned to the reed fields. Baby jumped into the water, and Sprout went to take a look at their nest. But then she saw something awful. The reed warblers had been attacked. Their nest was torn to shreds and broken shells were everywhere. The eggs had been just about to hatch! Their mother was gone. The male warbler wept as he circled above the reed fields. Sprout shuddered. As she left, she vowed not to make a permanent home anywhere. She would spot the hunter's shadow before the hunter spotted them.

JOINING THE BRACE

Along stretch of summer rain brought an enormous amount of water. The reservoir was so high that the reeds were almost completely submerged. These were difficult days for Sprout. It was hard to find a dry place, and because her feathers were always damp, she suffered from a continuous cold. She had become very thin because they changed nests every day and she didn't sleep well at night. Still, Baby was growing and looking quite duckish, a little more like Straggler every day. That pleased and amazed Sprout to no end. "Baby" wasn't fitting for an adolescent duck, so she named him Greentop, after his coloring. But she still liked to call him Baby, as that made her feel closer to him.

When the rains passed, Sprout finally fought off the cold that had plagued her. But it seemed unlikely that her scrawny body would ever be plump again. She was getting old. Of course she was: her baby was almost fully grown! Yet she was stronger than ever. Her calm eyes could detect the slightest movement in the darkness, her beak was hard, and her claws were sharp. Sprout and Greentop never spent more than two nights in one spot. Sometimes, from a distance, they saw the weasel returning home empty-jawed. Life as a wanderer was difficult, but it wasn't too bad. It did break Sprout's heart to see Greentop with a brooding expression on his face. He had become moody from time to time after the leader had visited them in the reeds. These episodes recurred more frequently after his feathers changed color. Sprout asked him what was wrong, but he wouldn't confide in her.

There wouldn't be rain again for a while. The stars twinkled at twilight, and Sprout's feathers remained dry overnight. With the nicer weather, Sprout and Greentop could find a place to sleep close to the water, but Sprout led Greentop up the slope to stay away from the weasel. She checked under the rock at the edge of the hill. They had slept in that small cave a few times during the rains, but Greentop didn't like it there because it was far from the reservoir.

"We haven't seen the hunter in two days. I'm sure we'll see him today. I bet he'll go around the reed fields to try to get at least a warbler," Sprout said, but Greentop wasn't listening. Deep in thought again, he was standing in a field of white daisy fleabane and looking down at the reservoir. He was just like his father. Sprout curled up in the cave and watched Greentop. He was no longer a baby. Even when she imagined talking to the mallard about what was going on with Greentop, she couldn't come up with a good solution. She was afraid the weasel would snatch Greentop like he did Straggler. It was dangerous when you let down your guard. She decided to call Greentop inside. Stepping out of the cave, she glimpsed a dark shadow slip down from a rock. It sounded like the wind but wasn't.

Sprout stopped breathing. It was the weasel.

How had she made this mistake? She had chosen the wrong spot. Until now they had managed to avoid the weasel, but he was one step ahead of them. Greentop wasn't paying any attention. Sprout had to take charge of the situation. She was his mother; she couldn't let this happen. Drawing in a deep breath, she sprinted out of the cave like lightning, clucking and flapping her wings, shouting, "Get lost!"

The weasel spun around. Greentop, taken by surprise, flapped his wings and screamed. Flustered, the weasel looked back at Greentop before turning to face Sprout. He looked bigger and swifter than before, but Sprout knew she couldn't back down. Greentop kept flapping his wings in fright. Sprout tensed her claws and raised all her feathers on end. Her eyes met the weasel's. "Don't you dare!" she threatened, prepared to die.

The weasel slowly shook his head, his eyes still trained on her. "Don't you interfere!" His voice gave Sprout the chills. The weasel wanted only Greentop, and so he wasn't wary of her.

Sprout glared at the weasel. "Leave my baby alone!"

The weasel laughed derisively. Sprout felt her heart pound and her entire body inflame with rage. She was no longer frightened by the weasel's stare. As the weasel was about to turn away, Sprout sprinted toward him like a moth darting toward a flame. She pecked viciously. The weasel screamed and sprang toward Greentop. Sprout, her beak firmly clamped on the weasel, was dragged along. She could hear Greentop making a racket. Sprout and the weasel became one and rolled down the slope. The writhing weasel clawed at Sprout's belly. Only when they hit a rock midslope did they become untangled. Sprout began to lose consciousness. "Run away, Baby," she coughed out. A moment later she opened her eyes. She couldn't see or move. Something was in her mouth. When she spat it out she realized it was a piece of flesh. The weasel's flesh. "Baby! Baby!" Sprout looked around. It was too quiet. Had the weasel gotten him? Was Greentop already dead? Tears sprang to her eyes. If Greentop was no longer, it would be harder to bear than her aching wounds. That awful beast! *He should have taken me. Baby is too young to go.* . . . Sprout closed her eyes. She was drained of energy, like the time she had been tossed into the Hole of Death.

"Mom, get up!"

Sprout felt a breeze overhead. She blinked. Greentop

was hovering in the air, flapping his wings. He was struggling to stay aloft, but he was definitely flying. "My goodness! What happened to your wings?"

"Isn't it amazing? I just needed to get away, and then I floated up. I can fly!" Greentop shouted with elation. Sprout couldn't speak. She just smiled. It was a miracle, the third she'd witnessed since leaving the coop and hatching Baby. This was the cherry on top! "Mom, let me see. Are you in pain?" Greentop spread his wings and embraced her. Sprout's throat closed up in gratitude. She set her beak firmly to hold back her tears, but that day it was impossible.

As summer waned, a dry wind began to blow. The sun's strong rays streamed from above, and the reed flowers began to wilt. This was a lonely time for Sprout. Greentop, caught up in the joys of flying, spent entire days at the reservoir. Sprout would walk along the reed fields or go up the slope to watch him swim and fly. The weasel didn't show himself. Perhaps he was back to peering into the chicken coops for chicks or hunting chickens on the brink of expiration in the Hole of Death, as he should have done all along. It was silly to salivate over Greentop. How could he think snatching a flying wild duck from the sky would be as easy as nabbing a fledgling in the yard?

Greentop loved flying. Not only did he stop worrying about the weasel, but he could also go from one end of the reservoir to the other in an instant. And he could coast above the reed fields to pick out a good sleeping place. His world expanded, from the ground and water to the sky. While Sprout envied Greentop, she missed him. He was her baby, but he was also a wild duck. *We chickens gave up on our wings. How is it that we are proud only of the fact that we are members of the comb? Combs are useless against hunters.*

Greentop was lonely like his mother. His mother was a hen, and yet he couldn't cluck. The barnyard ducks looked down on him. They refused to come near him or even acknowledge him. At the very least Sprout and Greentop's nights were nice—two lonely beings away from their kind, falling asleep pressed together. Sprout ate the fish Greentop brought every night and thought about the mallard, especially when her baby's sleek feathers glistened in the moonlight.

"Baby," she said one night, "even when you're sleeping, always keep your ears open. The hunter comes under cover of night. He will come at some point. He never gives up."

"Don't worry about me. I'm worried about you, Mom. You can't fly or swim."

"I'm fine. He isn't interested in me. I'm so lean he sees nothing appetizing about me," Sprout joked, touched that Greentop was concerned about her.

Greentop was silent for a moment. "Mom, I've been thinking," he said with difficulty. He was quiet again for a while. Sprout grew nervous. "How about we go back to the barn? I don't like being by myself all the time."

Sprout's heart sank. This was the first time he'd said something like that. He must have been wrestling with these feelings for a long time. "Back to the barn?"

"I'm a duck anyway. All I can do is quack."

"So what? Even though we look different, we cherish each other. I love you so much." Sprout parroted what the mallard had told her a long time ago. She'd understood the mallard, so she hoped Greentop would understand her.

But Greentop shook his head. "I don't know, Mom. What if the ducks never accept me? I want to be one of them." He started to weep.

Sprout didn't know what to do. She rubbed his back. "Baby, we've been fine so far. You're so smart, you learned how to swim and fly all on your own...." Sprout knew her words didn't help. Maybe she'd overreacted to the farmer's conversation with his wife. If his wings had been clipped, Greentop would have been one of the ducks. Perhaps she should have sent him along with the other ducks when the leader asked her to give him up.

"I know you love me. But we're still not the same kind," Greentop said.

"Right, we look different. But I'm so happy to have you. No matter what anyone says, you're still my baby," Sprout said, feeling sad.

Greentop moved away. "Mom, we need to go back. I'm going to join the brace."

"Then I'll be headed to the chicken coop. . . ." Sprout's heart sank. She didn't have the heart to scold him. Long ago, when Greentop fearlessly skipped across the lily pads and swam, Sprout realized he wasn't her kind. "Baby, I was a hen who had to lay eggs in a coop," she said gently, trying to dissuade him. "I've never been able to hatch my own egg, even though all I wanted to do was to sit on an egg and see the birth of a chick. When I couldn't lay any more eggs, I was taken out of the coop. I was fated to die. But when I met you, I finally became a mother." Greentop buried his head under his wing and didn't move. The soft moonlight glimmered on the water. "Baby, we don't have any reason to return to the barn. I'm not wanted there, and you're much better than any of those animals." Sprout stroked Greentop's back. Greentop didn't open his eyes or raise his head, although he heard everything she said. He had grown too big for her to embrace, even if she spread out her wings. Her baby had grown up too fast.

Sprout was restless all night. She didn't know what to do. She was useless now, even as a protector, since the weasel didn't come looking for them anymore. And even if he did, Greentop was strong enough to flee on his own. At dawn, when Greentop left for the reservoir, she didn't raise her head. She was afraid he would insist on joining the brace of ducks. From the slope she watched him sidling up to them. They were cold to him. They yelled at him. The leader even attacked him. But Greentop kept hanging around. As the sun set, the ducks returned to the yard.

Greentop trailed them. It was like watching the lonely mallard all over again.

"Baby, come back!" Sprout called. But nobody looked her way. "You'll be lonely in the yard. You're so special! The yard animals won't accept you." She followed him from a distance.

TRAVELERS FROM
ANOTHER WORLD

Sprout settled in the hills where she could see the yard. Nothing had changed—the faint light that seeped out of the chicken coop where the hens clucked loudly, the wheelbarrow of feed, the animals in the barn. Actually, there was one new thing: a cockerel. He was the one young chicken who had managed to avoid the weasel. Sprout couldn't see what was going on inside the barn, but she could guess. The ducks would be arguing about Greentop. Since the leader of the ducks didn't seem too thrilled to welcome him into the brace, Greentop might be chased away. Sprout thought that might be for the best. She wanted to take him back to the reservoir. Even if he was alone, at least he wouldn't be humiliated, and he would be able to fly freely.

The night passed. Greentop wasn't kicked out. The brace of ducks stuck their heads in the trough to eat, and Greentop ate from a smaller bucket. The farmer's wife had arranged that for him. It was clear she wanted him there. Anyone would, with his glistening feathers and beautiful form. If she wanted him, the rooster and the leader of the ducks would be forced to let him live in the barn. The ducks went off for a walk, with the leader at the head and the young ones trailing behind. When Greentop went to follow the young ducks, the farmer's wife grabbed him. He quacked in fright and flapped his wings. Sprout sprang to her feet. The ducks ignored the ruckus and continued on toward the reservoir. The farmer's wife tied Greentop to one of the wooden stilts elevating the chicken coop. He tried to escape but couldn't. He burst into tears, as did Sprout. No matter how hard he flapped his wings, he couldn't free himself from the cord. Sprout should have told him why they'd left the yard in the first place. Then he wouldn't have gone back. She couldn't sit still. Struggling to free himself, Greentop refused all food. The rooster family strolled into the garden, and the dog snoozed. In the evening the ducks returned, and everyone went into the barn to sleep.

Sprout hung around the perimeter of the yard. She wanted to go up to Greentop and stroke his back.

"Still alive? You're a tenacious one," the dog growled through his bared teeth.

Sprout glared at him fiercely. "You think I survived out of luck? I've experienced it all. You better not bother me."

"Ha! So confident. Well, you did raise a duckling. But don't even think about coming into the yard. I'm a strict gatekeeper, so I have the habit of biting first." He sauntered back into his house.

From under the acacia tree, Sprout called to Greentop, "Baby, Mom's here. Don't cry. We'll figure something out."

"Mom, don't leave me here! My leg, it hurts!"

Her nerves on edge, Sprout paced around. The farmer and his wife hadn't tied up Straggler. So why Baby? Still pacing, she approached the Hole of Death without realizing it.

Sprout sensed something insidious. In the darkness, something glared at her. The weasel. But he had only one glinting eye. Sprout puffed out her neck feathers and tensed her claws. Her blood boiling, she was ready to go on the offensive. The weasel had a dying chicken between his jaws. Sprout could detect the twitching of a wing. The weasel approached her slowly, and she didn't retreat. He wouldn't get her while he had dinner in his jaws. He set the chicken down but didn't crouch to attack. Sprout puffed out her chest and glared at him.

"A delectable duck," the weasel sneered. "I'll get him before long!" He laughed menacingly.

"You'll never get him!"

"No? Even though he's tied to that stilt? Soon he'll be so fat he won't be able to fly. That's how they get tame." Again the weasel laughed. Sprout suddenly understood. Straggler wasn't tied down because his wing was damaged; he couldn't fly away. "And you!" the weasel hissed. "You blinded me in one eye! I'll get you back. Both of you, soon enough."

Sprout was astonished. That piece of flesh in her mouth

had been the weasel's eye! "I'd rather drown in the reservoir than let you devour me," she shot back.

"Don't do that. I don't like eating dead chickens. Stay alive and just watch what I do to your baby!" The weasel laughed yet again. He grabbed his chicken and disappeared into the darkness. Sprout stared after him. She had goose bumps and was trembling. The weasel had put a curse on her. She shook her head to clear it and left the Hole of Death. She couldn't forget his words. Would he come into the yard, even with the gatekeeper there? The dog would go crazy, and so would the other animals. *He's going to attack my baby.* But Greentop was tied up; the weasel couldn't possibly snatch him away. *He'll bide his time until Greentop is too plump to fly, and wait for the farmer's wife to untie the knot.*

The next day the weasel sauntered into view and went directly to the Hole of Death. But he returned empty-jawed. He crept toward the yard where the cockerel was digging in the compost pile. The weasel knew Sprout was watching from the hill. Tauntingly he turned toward her. Sprout was frozen in place. She wanted to yell and warn the cockerel, but nothing came out. The dog didn't sense anything; his nose and ears must have become dulled with age. Sprout was sure the weasel was trying to intimidate her. Suddenly Greentop started to holler. With his good hearing he had sensed danger before anyone else. Everything happened all at once. The dog barked in the same instant the weasel shot forward like an arrow and the cockerel shrieked. Barking furiously, the dog chased the dark shadow, and the animals scurried out of the barn. The farmer and his wife came out last. The cockerel was nowhere to be found. The rooster couple clucked and clucked, looking everywhere for their baby. Quacking with alarm, the ducks joined the chorus.

"That damn weasel!" said the farmer. His wife, who was trying to herd the ducks back into the barn, answered, "We need a bulldog—that dog's too old. Otherwise the native chicken seed will dry up."

"The weasel came because you tied up that duck!" snapped the farmer. "It's like inviting him to a dinner party. Go tie it up in the barn!"

Sprout paced nervously as she watched the farmer's wife untie the cord then drag Greentop, quacking and squirming, into the barn by his foot. Sprout couldn't keep an eye on him if he was tied up inside. She wouldn't be able to forgive herself. "Let go of my baby!" Sprout clucked as she barreled toward her. The farmer's wife was astonished at the sight of a hen flapping at her. Like a fighting cock's, Sprout's feathers stood on end as she pecked at the farmer's wife.

"Ow! Ow! This damn chicken's going to kill me!" the farmer's wife hollered. All the ducks came out of the barn, quacking. Another huge ruckus ensued. In trying to shoo away Sprout, the farmer's wife lost her grip on Greentop.

"Baby! Fly away!" Sprout shouted, and Greentop lifted off powerfully. With the cord still dangling from his leg, he disappeared behind the hill. The other ducks stared in awe. Sprout ran off, just cheating death as the farmer's wife swung a broom at her. The path to the reservoir was long and dark. But Sprout had nothing to fear. In fact she was so delighted she couldn't help humming. The poor cockerel had filled the weasel's belly, and Greentop would no longer want to stay in the yard. He'd learned a valuable lesson. *Just because you're the same kind doesn't mean you're all one happy family. The important thing is to understand each other. That's love!* Sprout ran on, elated, bursting into song.

Sprout was thinner than ever. She ate only to stave off hunger and spent all her time running around looking for Greentop, so she'd gotten as small as a reed warbler. After escaping the yard, Greentop chose to nest alone. He didn't come back to Sprout, not even at night; he stayed at the reservoir. Sprout was able to see him from afar, but she didn't know where he was sleeping. She missed falling asleep nestled against him and talking to him. But there was nothing she could do about the situation—she knew it was hard for him to accept that they were not the same kind. But Sprout wanted to help him get rid of the cord tied to his foot. It trailed him wherever he went, and he looked downcast, as though it was sorrow that trailed him. Greentop didn't want Sprout near him, but Sprout made her bed where she could see him. Although the weasel lurked now and then, Greentop had excellent hearing, as did Sprout, so they always knew when he was near.

Autumn passed slowly. In the reed fields Sprout began to spot dragonflies who had laid eggs on the water plants in what would be their final flight. After they landed, their wings stiffened, and their many eyes gazed up at the blue sky. Their eyes still moved, but they didn't harbor fear when Sprout approached to eat them. She didn't particularly enjoy eating these large-eyed, slender dragonflies, so she helped herself only when famished. The sun began to set earlier, causing the ducks to return from the reservoir sooner, leaving only the sound of the wind and the dry rustling of grass to echo in the reed fields. Greentop swam until late, then dragged his long cord into the reed fields. Sprout slowly followed him as the cold autumn night settled in.

One early morning the wind blew mightily, shaking the reed fields. Something was in the air. Sprout trembled as the wind cut into her feathers. She became worried about Greentop, who was within shouting distance. "Baby, are you okay?"

Greentop was looking around nervously, his neck outstretched. He suddenly shouted, "Mom, be careful!" and flew into the air. Sprout tensed up. Greentop signaled that the weasel was near, then circled the reed fields making a ruckus. "There are three—wait, there's another! Why are there so many?"

Sprout panicked. One was enough to deal with, but now there were four! She cautiously emerged from the reed fields. Out of nowhere the one-eyed weasel appeared. He snorted at her. Sprout glared back.

"You're not what we're looking for—unless there's nothing else to eat in the fields," the weasel said with a mischievous smile. He turned around.

Sprout snapped back: "Only an excellent hunter can catch him. For a one-eyed hunter like you, it's got to be hard enough just to keep him in view. You came with three others, but look, he's up in the air! Or maybe you haven't spotted him yet because you're missing an eye?"

Annoyed, the weasel crouched and bared his teeth. But he didn't attack. "It's hunting season. Finally! We've been waiting for this!" And off he ran.

Sprout looked around. It was overcast. Each time a gust of wind blew, the reeds collapsed and then wearily staggered up. The rough wind that felled the reeds left a large footprint. Something extraordinary was about to occur. Greentop called to Sprout, and Sprout called back. Having completed a loop around the reservoir, he landed next to her. For the first time in a long while, they stood side by side and looked down at the reservoir together.

"Mom, it's strange. I've never felt like this before. Something is about to happen."

"Hunters?"

"No, not that."

"Is it something more frightening?"

"Mom, this is different. It's covering the entire sky. Can't you feel it?"

"Baby, what are you talking about?" Sprout couldn't tell what Greentop was seeing through his squinted eyes or what he was hearing.

"Wow, that sound! Mom, it's amazing. So many of them are flocking this way!"

She couldn't tell what was about to happen, but she knew it was going to be entirely new. As she waited, she started to feel it. The noise reverberated between the sky and the mountains far away. It gradually expanded, getting louder. And finally black spots appeared.

They were birds, countless birds that soon covered the sky. The entire world filled with birds, and Sprout couldn't hear anything else. The birds circled the reservoir and started landing on the water. Sprout and Greentop gaped at the travelers from another world.

"Straggler! Your family is here!" Sprout whispered. They had to be his kind, the family he'd missed every time he struggled to climb the hill to look far off in the distance. He'd been separated from such a big flock—how lonely he must have been without them!

"Mom, why is my heart pounding so hard?" Greentop buried his head in Sprout's wing, like he'd done as a baby. He was trembling, inexplicably moved.

"Of course it is! You've never seen such a beautiful flock." Sprout felt at peace. She smiled. *Ah, old friend! Now I understand everything.* She'd thought she understood when Straggler had told her to go to the reservoir with the baby. But she hadn't. He'd wanted Greentop to grow up and fly away, following his own kind. Sprout opened her wings and held her grown baby close. She embraced him for a long time. Feeling his silky feathers and taking in his scent, she stroked his back. This might be the last time. Precious moments did not remain forever. Sprout wanted to sear all this into her memory. Memories would soon be all she had.

THE BONE-WEARY,
ONE-EYED HUNTER

Straggler was right: The one-eyed weasel was larger and faster than the other weasels. He was meticulous and swift, sometimes teaming up with another weasel for the hunt. The weasels hung around the reservoir, biding their time. They were targeting the mallard ducks. They snatched young ducks separated from the flock or those who'd come on their maiden voyage. The mallard ducks slept in a cluster in the reed fields and swam in a group. When the leader flew up, they all followed, creating an awe-inspiring din. The quiet reservoir had awakened. Greentop left Sprout to join them, but they weren't interested in him. Having grown up in the fields, he didn't have to worry about smelling like a domestic duck, but the cord around his foot gave the impression that he had run away from a human, so the wild ducks were wary of him.

Sprout didn't leave the slope. She was safe there—the weasels targeted only the mallard ducks, and the slope was the best place from which to look down on the reed fields. Greentop tried very hard to be accepted. Even though the mallard ducks didn't give him a passing glance, he tagged along and slept with them. He didn't mind making his bed at the far edge of the group, where it was the most dangerous. It was difficult to have to watch Greentop sitting apart from the flock or swimming alone, but there was nothing Sprout could do to help him. To her, he had always been special, especially compared to the domestic ducks. But he couldn't fly as well as the mallards—he was slower and didn't have their stamina. The cord was to blame; Sprout wished she could cut it off. She spent her days searching for stray grains in the straw piles of the rice paddies, and in the evening she returned to the cave on the slope. The cave under the rock was cozy, insulating her from the frost. From there she tracked the weasels as they roamed the reed fields. She could tell those rascals were up to no good.

By the time autumn turned to winter, the weasels had eaten all the young and weak mallards. Now, after the first snow, their hunts were less successful. Healthy mallards were formidable opponents. The hungry weasels were swift on their tails, but they were lucky to get one every other day. If they managed to catch one, they growled and snapped at one another, fighting for a larger share. Two of them left for better hunting grounds, but the one-eyed weasel remained with a friend.

Sprout was concerned about Greentop, since he slept at the edge of the group. In a hunt, Greentop would be the first attacked. And he'd be dragged down by that cumbersome cord around his foot. *Baby, sleep lightly to-*

night. They've been hungry for two days. Standing on the slope, Sprout watched the weasels as they hid in a pile of fallen reeds. The mallards were still swimming. Snow began to fall. And Sprout paced. Flakes piled on the reed fields and the dry grass where the weasels were hiding. One by one the mallards emerged to groom themselves. At the leader's signal they all flew up, circled the reservoir, and flew over the hill. They sometimes found a good spot over there, but more often they returned to the reed fields. Sprout squinted, trying to make out Greentop. In the snow she couldn't see the hanging cord, and without it even Sprout couldn't recognize her baby. She knew he would keep his ears open—he was well versed in how the hunters operated—but she was still anxious.

Sprout settled in her cave. She hoped the flock would choose to sleep elsewhere—in the straw piles of the rice paddies or the thickets in the hills. She hadn't eaten because she was too busy monitoring the weasels, but she was okay. She was used to eating very little or nothing at all; it suited her, if not her weight and feathers. The snowfall turned heavy. A snowdrift piled up at the entrance to the cave and blocked her sight, but she could still hear everything. The weasels were half-crazed from hunger. She remembered how Straggler would stay up all night dancing and shouting. He had done everything he could to protect the egg. *I'm his mother. I can't sit back and let him get caught.* Sprout pushed through the snow and stepped outside.

The flock of mallard ducks was returning. They must have decided to bed down in the reed fields again. They would find a spot with thick reeds to escape the snow, but the weasels were already hiding there. After circling the gray sky they would settle into their sleeping spots. Sprout had to hurry. She ran down the slope, but snow poured down on her, forcing her to close her eyes. When she opened them, Greentop was standing in front of her; his strong wings had scattered the snow over her.

"Baby!" She was thrilled. She opened her wings in greeting.

Greentop looked tired and sad. Suddenly a ruckus started up in the reed fields, and the brace rose up at once. Greentop ran to the edge of the slope. "A hunt!" Sprout and Greentop listened attentively to the brief scream that pierced the darkness. The weasels would be full tonight. A sacrificed life meant a peaceful night for the group. Sprout was grateful that Greentop was safe.

Greentop leaned his head against Sprout. "I can't stand it. I just want to live with you, Mom. Other ducks my age sleep in the inner circle, surrounded by the adults. But I have to sleep on the outside, farther out than the lookout. When we fly, I don't know where I'm supposed to be. When I'm next to an adult, I'm scolded for being rude, and if I'm behind them, they make fun of me. I'm always a loner, wherever I am. Why do I have to live like this? I'm done. I'm happiest when I'm with you, Mom. That's why I came back."

Judging from his thin body, Greentop had clearly had a difficult time with the mallards. But his wings could now create wind—he really was a wild duck now. Tired, Greentop went inside the cave, dragging the long cord behind him. His footprints and the line from the cord were stamped on the snow.

"Sleep well," Sprout whispered as her baby curled up in a ball.

The snow piled up and blocked the entrance to the cave once more, making it warm inside. Greentop started to snore, but Sprout couldn't sleep. Tonight she had to rid him of the cord. All night she pecked at it. By the time morning came around she was dizzy, and her beak was so sore she couldn't even open it. But the cord was now ragged; it could easily snap off. Greentop woke up. His eyes welled at the sight of the frayed cord. He grabbed one end with his bill, and Sprout grabbed the other. They each pulled, and the cord finally ripped apart. Because Sprout wasn't able to undo the knot, a piece of the cord remained, like a ring around his foot, but Greentop didn't find it bothersome. Exhausted and sore, Sprout lay down. Greentop lingered quietly before clearing the snow from the entrance to the cave and going outside. As she fell asleep, Sprout watched him fly away.

Some time passed.

"Mom, wake up," Greentop said, shaking Sprout awake. Sprout pried her eyes open. Greentop had brought her a delectable fish. His eyes widened as he said, "Do you know who the victims were? Two of them. One was the guide who looks for places to sleep, and the other was the lookout!"

The weasels must have attacked in desperation, pouncing on those who landed first rather than waiting for a better opportunity. Sprout ate the fish. If it hadn't been for Greentop, she wouldn't have been able to enjoy such a wonderful meal in the middle of winter. "Thank you, Baby. It was delicious."

Greentop grinned. Sprout smiled, but she felt sad. "I'm so glad I was able to free you of that cord. But I can't do anything about the ring around your foot. Let's just leave it as a marker that you're my baby. So that I can recognize you among the travelers."

"Mom, do you want me to leave?"

Sprout looked into Greentop's eyes and nodded. "You should leave. Don't you think you should follow your kind and see other worlds? If I could fly I would never stay here. I don't know how I could live without you. But you should leave. Go become the lookout. Nobody has better hearing than you."

"I won't leave," Greentop said tearfully, burying his head in Sprout's wing.

"Do what you want to do. Ask yourself what that is."

"You'll be by yourself. And you can't go back to the barnyard."

"I'll be fine. I have many good memories to keep me company."

Greentop cried quietly, and Sprout stroked his back.

She wanted to tell him to try harder to be accepted by the brace, but she couldn't talk through the lump in her throat.

"They might change the sleeping spot because of the hunters. I heard they may go to the mountains on the other side of the water, but then I may not be able to see you for a long time," Greentop mumbled. Sprout listened quietly— she knew he would join them, and she was proud of him. Still, knowing that his heart had never completely left the brace, she felt empty. It was difficult to remain on her feet. "You and I look different, Mom, but I love you regardless," Greentop said, then rushed out of the cave.

Sprout stood still, unable to move. Greentop looked back. She hurried after him, but he was already flying. He circled the cave once and then headed to the reservoir. Sprout stood on the slope, watching him return to his kind. She felt like a mere shell of herself.

Winter was nearing its end. In the shade, snow remained unmelted, but in sunny spots mugwort and daisy fleabane were starting to surface. Sprout was thrilled to taste the new greens, even though they were slightly frozen. She spent the remainder of winter on the move—the weasel had become even more desperate from hunger. She moved from the reed fields to the cave, from under a fallen tree to the straw piles of the rice paddy and then to a rotten row-boat, taking care not to cross paths with the weasel. Her favorite spot was the straw pile housing bugs that could fill her belly, but she couldn't stay long, since many field mice and fleas lived there as well. After the old dog was sold and a bulldog was stationed by the coop as the new gatekeeper, the weasel's hunger became particularly acute. As the number of prey declined, the other weasel left. But not the one-eyed one.

Even after they lost the guide and the lookout, the mallards continued to make their bed in the reed fields. For the weasel stalking through the snow-covered fields, mallard ducks were a rich source of protein he couldn't give up. The lookout was the one duck the weasel had a chance of catching. So Greentop remained the weasel's target. He was now a respected lookout, with his thundering voice, glistening coat, and powerful wings. Nobody shunned him anymore. When the mallard ducks settled away from the reservoir at night, the weasel hunted for Sprout. Despite the lack of feathers and fat on her body, she was the best catch in the fields. But the weasel kept missing her; for some reason he had slowed down.

The wind turned warmer. The ice on the reservoir melted, and the mallard ducks swam with vigor. Sprout ambled along the edge of the reservoir to watch Greentop from up close. The barnyard ducks came out for their first spring swim—they hadn't been able to swim all winter, so they jumped in clamorously as soon as they reached the water. The leader greeted Sprout with sympathy. "You must have had a difficult winter—you've lost too much weight!" Sprout just smiled; she wasn't all that envious of the ducks, who had grown fat in the barn over the winter. "But you look good," the leader said in a generous spirit. "What I mean is, your appearance isn't too good, but something . . ." He shrugged. "You seem different from our hen. It's odd: you're more confident and graceful, even though you're missing some feathers." Sprout took that as a compliment. Grooming his feathers before entering the water, the leader asked, "Where's the duckling? Did he . . ." He was asking if Greentop had died. Sprout pointed as Greentop took flight powerfully. Surprised, the leader squinted to watch. He gave a little bow of respect. Pleased, Sprout meandered away from the reed fields.

As she passed a small weeping willow, Sprout heard strange noises coming from the dry grass around it. She listened carefully. They were the cries of babies, weak but frantic. Sprout pushed her face into the dry grass. It was dark, and she couldn't see anything. When her eyes grew accustomed to the darkness, she realized she was in a small cave. Tiny young babies were squirming, their bodies pressed against one another, not yet able to open their eyes. Who were they? Whose were they? Sprout's heart pounded.

They were four-legged babies.

Sprout turned around and left. It wouldn't do her any good if she were suspected of doing something to them. But she was curious. Where was their mother? These babies were too young to open their eyes; wouldn't they die without her? Sprout climbed the slope and waited to see if she could catch a glimpse of the mother heading to the cave. But nobody came. It was late. The barnyard ducks left the reservoir, and the mallards flew up. But no mother headed for the babies. Sprout was worried. Was the mother dead? Then who would raise the babies?

Sprout came to her senses when the mallards returned from flying over the mountain. They were flying close for once, and so Sprout looked out at the reed fields, hoping to spot Greentop. What she noticed was the weasel—he was hiding in the thicket, just like the day he had snatched the guide and the lookout. Sprout tensed up: Greentop was in danger. It had been a while since she'd last seen the weasel. If he'd gone hungry the entire time, he'd be desperate. The mallards circled the reservoir. Sprout didn't have time to waste. She sprinted down the slope, flapping her wings. If only she could fly instead of having to depend on her stubby legs to run along the ground! These useless, useless wings! "You awful creature!" Sprout shouted at the weasel as she started to tumble down the slope. Dry grass and trees clawed at her mercilessly, but she didn't feel a thing. Her only thought was to get to the reed fields before Greentop landed. "Look here! Here I come!" she bellowed. She must have looked silly, a ball of tangled feathers and straw, but her voice was beyond ferocious.

The weasel got up immediately. He approached her, growling, his eyes glinting with rage. Sprout faced him defiantly. The weasel was so thin, Sprout almost felt bad for him. How long had he been starving? He didn't look like the hunter he once was, who moved like the wind. Then

she glimpsed his distended stomach and nipples. *Oh!*
Sprout was stunned. In the depths of winter she'd wondered how the weasel's belly had grown so round. And why
he'd been so slow. But now she understood: the four-legged
babies whining in hunger in the hidden cave—the weasel
was their mother!

The mallards were about to land. One duck landed
first. Sprout saw the cord around his foot. Greentop.

"You annoying hen! Get lost!" The weasel bared her
teeth.

Sprout had to distract her somehow. She took a step
back and warned, "Watch out. I'm going to your babies!"
And she sprinted toward the willow tree.

Realizing after a moment what was going on, the weasel
dashed after her. Sprout ran with her beak clenched. No
matter how weak the weasel was, she was still an excellent
hunter. Sprout was nearly nabbed by the neck but got to
the cave under the willow tree first. With her claws, she
grabbed the babies that were huddled together. They were
mere chunks of flesh, still furless. Sprout really didn't want
to do this—it wasn't right—but there was no other way.
With her single eye, the weasel looked pleadingly at Sprout.
They stared at each other until their breathing calmed. The
babies wailed at Sprout's feet. The weasel's expression
crumpled pathetically at their cries. "Please, be merciful,"
the weasel pleaded, her voice trembling. "They haven't even
opened their eyes yet."

Sprout shook her head. "You could have been merciful

many times. But you weren't. Not to the white duck, not to Straggler, not to me or my baby. You had many chances, but you never were!"

"I couldn't help it. You just happened to be around when I was hungry. I did it so I wouldn't starve."

"We just happened to be around? No, you couldn't wait to eat us up. Now I'll hurt your precious babies! That's only fair."

"No, no, that's not fair. You're not hungry. I hunt only when I'm hungry. To survive."

"I've spent my entire life running away from you. You have no idea how exhausted and sad I've been."

"I don't believe it!" the weasel retorted. "You're the luckiest hen alive! I've never been able to catch you. You've done so many things. I'm the exhausted one. I've got blisters on my feet from following you around so much."

Sprout thought for a moment. The weasel wasn't entirely wrong. Sprout had almost died many times, but here she was, still alive. She felt bad for the young babies pressed under her sharp claws. Their soft skin would bleed in an instant. She unclenched her claws gradually so the weasel wouldn't notice. "If you find another source of food, will you leave my baby alone?"

"Of course!"

"Promise? If I told you where to find something to eat?"

The weasel nodded quickly. "I promise. If there's something else to eat, I won't go near your baby."

"I'm old, but my claws and beak are still strong," Sprout

warned. "You should know that from experience. If you don't keep your promise, your babies might lose an eye just like their mother." Then she told the weasel about the haystacks in the rice paddies, about the herd of field mice that had fattened up over the winter, fighting every night over their cramped quarters. The weasel's eye sparkled with joy, but she hesitated to leave the cave, not entirely trusting Sprout.

"You go first. Then I'll leave, too," Sprout promised.

The weasel finally left. Sprout took another look at the babies trembling in cold and in hunger. She felt pity for a fellow mother. A mother who ran through the dark fields; a mother who had to return quickly to her still-blind babies, who couldn't survive if she wasn't as swift as the wind; a mother who was a bone-weary, one-eyed hunter.

ALOFT LIKE A FEATHER

Green shoots sprouted from every place touched by sunlight. Yellow flowers bloomed on the cornelian cherry trees in the back hills. Spring had come. Sprout paced the rim of the reservoir every day. But Greentop never swam over to her. She understood that the lookout couldn't leave the pack, but she had a hard time suppressing her disappointment. It had been ages since they last spoke.

The pleasant weather took a sudden turn for the worse. The wind was cold, the sky overcast, threatening snow. Sprout didn't feel well. She was gray and gloomy, just like the weather. Exhausted after having walked along the reservoir all day, she returned to the slope. These days she returned to the cave on the slope every night so she could watch Greentop. She wanted to slow down in her old age. She knew the weasel was around, but she didn't have the energy to flee. Sprout started to empathize with the weasel. She knew how difficult it was to go through winter with someone to care for. Sprout crouched at the end of the slope and faced down the cold winds. Sometimes a feather would loosen and blow away. The fierce wind gouged her flesh, but she didn't feel like going inside. Overcome with lethargy, she squinted down at the reservoir. She didn't think she'd make it down there the next day.

In the afternoon the brace of mallards became more active. When they surrounded the leaders and quacked loudly that day, they sounded more excited and louder than on any other day. Sprout didn't know they were preparing to leave for the winterlands up north. The wind blew harder. It cut loose from the back hills and roamed widely, raking the dry fields. Leaves flew about and reeds rustled. The mallards flapped their wings as the hungry weasel circled them, looking for an opportunity. The leader of the mallards took off powerfully into the air. The others flew behind him one by one, in rows. Sprout looked up at them as they circled the reservoir and the back hills. One broke away and flew down toward the slope. Sprout got to her feet. "Greentop, my baby!"

Sprout spread her wings to greet him, but instead of landing he circled briefly around her. Brushing her with his wings, he called, "Mom!" as if to say good-bye. The wind carried his voice into the fields. Sprout stood dumbly in the draft he'd created. She realized this was farewell. *He's leaving!* She'd always known this day would come. But she hadn't had enough time to talk to him or give him a proper good-bye. Greentop took off again and flapped powerfully to catch up to the other ducks, who were far away by now. Sprout released all the many things she had kept in her heart, waiting for the right moment to share with him. But they failed to become a single word; instead she could let out only sobs. *My baby is leaving me!*

The flock of mallards blanketed the sky and gradually disappeared beyond the mountains in the distance, their sound becoming faint. It was as though some unknowable world on the other side of the sky was drawing them in. Suddenly everything was too quiet. Sprout couldn't breathe. It hurt every time she tried, as though her heart were being dislodged. She desperately wanted to go with her baby. She wanted to fly alongside the mallards. She feared being left alone; she hated what was happening.

At some point the weasel had approached. But the hunter didn't frighten her as much as the prospect of being alone. Sprout closed her eyes. She'd had a single wish, to sit on an egg and see the birth of a baby. Her wish had come true. She'd had a hard life, but she'd been happy. That was what had sustained her. *Now I want to fly away! I want to go far away like Greentop!* She flapped her wings. Why hadn't she practiced, when even young Greentop started clumsily on his own? She'd never realized that she'd harbored another wish. It was more than a wish; it was something she physically longed for. Sprout stared into the empty sky, feeling terribly lonely. The weasel's eye was boring into her. But Sprout kept squinting and squinting, trying to look to the end of the sky. Snow began to fall. As she watched snowflakes drifting in the wind, a smile spread across her face. *The acacia flowers are falling!* To Sprout, the snow looked just like acacia petals. Wanting to feel the falling

petals with her entire being, she spread her wings wide.
She wanted to smell them. She felt wonderful. She wasn't
cold or lonely anymore.

Then, a snarl, and everything disappeared—the petals
of the acacia flowers, the scent, the gentle breeze. In front
of Sprout was a starving weasel. "It's you," Sprout said,
looking into the weasel's sunken eye. She thought about
those soft babies and their delicate flesh. They were like the
last egg she laid, the one with a soft shell that had shattered
in the yard. Sprout remembered how her heart had broken, how sad she'd felt. Her body was stiff now. No longer
could she run away. She no longer had reason to, nor did
she have the energy. "Go on, eat me," she urged. "Fill your
babies' bellies." She closed her eyes.

Sprout was suffocating. She had imagined it would
hurt, but now all she felt was bone-deep relief. *You got me,
finally.* Everything turned black. She'd experienced this
once before in the fields. When she'd heard the white duck
scream. Everything had turned black, and then, very gradually, as now, she'd sensed a reddish hue. Then everything
slowly became brighter.

Sprout opened her eyes. The sky was a blinding blue.
She felt transparent and buoyant. And then, like a feather,
she was aloft. Gliding through the air with her large, beautiful wings, Sprout looked down at everything below—the
reservoir and the fields in a snowstorm, and the weasel
limping away, a scrawny hen dangling from her jaws.

Visit our website for a reading guide
and exclusive content on
The Hen Who Dreamed She Could Fly
www.oneworld-publications/hen